TH
SUSPE

BLACK AND WHITE

DAWN LEE MCKENNA

2019

A SWEET TEA PRESS PUBLICATION

First published in the United States by Sweet Tea Press

Edited by Debbie Maxwell Allen

Cover by Shayne Rutherford

wickedgoodbookcovers.com

Interior Design by Colleen Sheehan

ampersandbookinteriors.com

for

Hancy Deacon

I love you, my Hank

FOREWORD

I was born in Florida in 1963. In 1973, I was a good twenty years younger than the main characters in this book, but my memories of this time are exceptionally clear; in fact, the early seventies are the most vivid period in my memory.

Where I grew up, in South Florida and the Keys, neighborhoods were not divided so much by race as they were by economy. While most places did have one neighborhood referred to by the ignorant or old as "Colored Town", any poor or working poor neighborhood housed a mixture of blacks, Cubans and whites. We were working poor all of my life, and I thought the whole world was organized that way. In my world, it seemed normal that many of my friends were either black or Cuban.

I think this is why I have always bristled at the notion that the south was so clearly divided between white and everything else, that southern whites only loved each other, or that the place of your birth determined whether or not you were a racist.

Mind you, I'm not a revisionist by any means. The south bears the scars and the shame of hate. My point is that those scars and that hate were everywhere. At times, racism has been much more visible and evident in the south, and this has overshadowed the other side of the south, the south where your friends were determined by your neighborhood or economic class, not by the color of their skin.

All of my books are set in the south, most of them in Florida. And all of my books feature black characters who are not landscape dressing, but integral parts of the story. I never gave it much thought. It isn't some intentional effort to be inclusive. And it certainly isn't to show how enlightened and unbigoted I am.

It's because, to me, that's how life is populated. I cannot write about a life in the south where all of the vital characters are white, because I have no experience with it. I'm not talking about a southern life that includes blacks because they're there, in the background. For color, as it were. I'm talking about a southern life in which so many of the important characters happen to be black, because in my south, you were all part of the same economic class. For the record, yes, I do know that not all blacks were or are working poor. But I didn't know wealthy or middle-class black people, just as I didn't know the white people who had pools in their back yards or belonged to the country club.

I was an only, and unhappy, child. My ideals of family and home were shaped largely by the black and Cuban families I knew. Large families that socialized mainly with each other. Loud houses full of cousins and siblings and grandparents and music. Homes where the menu was made up of "poor people's" food, but there was always something going on the stove, and you were always expected to sit down and eat.

In this book, this series, you will meet people that I loved as a child. You'll meet Mama Tyne, who I loved in Key West. In a crowd of kids doing the bump while watching Soul Train, I was her "little white chile", the one who was too skinny, and who was never going to be black enough to dance well.

This isn't to say that I know about some magical, Disney movie south where everyone was openminded and it was normal for blacks and Cubans and whites to sit down to Thanksgiving dinner together. I also remember the violence and the hatred, the inexplicable desire to create a world that was either entirely black or entirely white.

The thing is, the south I knew, and the south that was on the news, were in the same place. Fairness, love and kindness were not relegated to Fort Lauderdale or Key West, and hatred and violence were not reserved for small towns like Dismal. Good and bad, black and white, love and hate, welcome and intolerance, existed throughout.

Dismal, Florida is not a real town, and yet it is. It's based on towns that you can still visit today. They're in the Panhandle, out near the Everglades, and half an hour away from Disney World. There are no Wal-Marts or amusement parks. They have tiny, deteriorating downtowns, and the grocery store is not part of a chain. There are boarded-up, weed-choked, one-story motels, with ten rooms and mid-century modern signs that say "Vacancy". They have a diner that is not adorable, and serves the best biscuits for miles around. Back in the 60s and 70s, they had people who hated, and people who loved, and those people were both black and white. They're dying out, but there are towns like Dismal all over Florida. The only thing I've made up is the name.

This book, and this series, is a departure from the others. It's set in a different time, and tackles some things that are hard. But like my other series, there is also humor, love, and fun.

I've always had an extremely detailed sensory memory. It has helped me, I suppose, to write in such a way that many readers say I can put them in a place or scene so vividly that it seems real. The sounds, the smells, the visual details. If you're too young to remember this period, I hope the details, my memories, will put you there. And if you lived it, I hope the details take you back.

The world is black, the world is white

Florida air is different; every Floridian knows that. To the beach town people, Atlantic or Gulf, Florida air is salty and soft, and even tourists notice the difference between the air in Fort Lauderdale and the air in Cincinnati.

But inland Florida, the air there isn't beach air. The air further inland is thick and heavy. If you hold your hand out the window as you drive, you can feel it move through your open fingers almost languidly. It's silky and dense, and smells of pine and dirt and, in some cases, swamp.

Someone born and bred in the inland areas of Florida can tell the difference in the air even five or ten miles south of the Alabama/Florida line, or at least they think they can, especially after a long time away.

Jennifer Sheehan could, and when she'd driven over the bridge from Mobile, she'd cranked her window all the way down. Her '66 Dodge Dart's air-conditioning hadn't been conditioning much for at least a couple of hours, anyway.

The heat had rushed in with the wind. For a moment, Jennifer felt a wave of moist warmth flood over her face and chest. Then the temperature in the car became the same as the temperature outside. She stuck her arm out the window and let the wind blow through her fingers, and breathed deeply.

She hadn't thought she'd missed the scent of Florida but, as soon as she smelled it, she knew she had. Suddenly, transposed over the view of the highway, were other images that were almost as real, and flew by almost as fast. Her mother hanging laundry, barefoot and wearing a blue dress. Herself at six, running through the sprinklers in her flowered romper. Drinking from Grandma's hose, so thirsty she drank it hot instead of waiting for it to cool off. She had sworn she could taste metal and rubber on her tongue.

Two lines of sweat had developed almost instantly beneath the rims of her sunglasses, and she'd pushed them up onto her head, squinting at the too-white sunlight. She had swiped at her cheeks, then pulled the glasses back down.

Now, an hour and a half later, she realized that she was only about forty-five minutes from her destination. She wasn't ready, and she was thirsty. She pulled into a Gulf station on her right. I-10 hadn't quite made it this far east, and US 90 was still a two-lane trip through the sticks. The last filling station had been a ways back, and there'd been a line, so she pulled up to one of the pumps. She had just grabbed her purse and gotten out of the car when a skinny guy in his early twenties appeared out of nowhere.

He wore tan coveralls that were embellished with grease stains, and he was wiping his hands on a shop towel. His red hair was receding early, and there was a smattering of freckles on his cheeks.

He smiled at her. "Fill 'er up, miss?"

"Yes, please." Jennifer's throat was dry, and her voice sounded funny to her after a full day of not speaking to anyone.

"Check your oil?" the guy asked, as he lifted the nozzle.

"No, thanks," she answered. "But could you check my water?"

"Sure thing," he answered. "Keys inside?"

She nodded at him. "Do you have a soda machine?"

"No, but there's a cooler inside. Twenty-five cents."

"Thanks." She stretched her back, pulled the hem of her red T-shirt back down.

"If you need to wash up, the ladies' room is in the back on the right," the man said. "You can get the key from Mike."

Jennifer nodded her thanks, then walked across the lot to the door. There were a couple of pickups parked out front, and an AMC station wagon parked in the open bay.

The bell above the door tinkled as she opened it, and cool air drifted out to greet her. It wasn't cold, but it was a lot better than the air outside.

There was a counter to her left with assorted fuses and hoses and other automotive needs. The wall behind it was covered with posters and car ads cut from magazines. Some of them went all the way back to what looked like the mid-fifties.

On her right was another counter with the cash register and some snacks. A countertop wire rack held dusty postcards from places that were at least fifty miles away. In the window behind that counter, the AC unit chugged and wheezed. It was assisted a bit by the green metal fan on the counter. The fan blew tendrils of dust out toward Jennifer.

At the end of the counter, two older men in ball caps and shirtsleeves leaned toward a transistor radio. On the other side of them sat a thin man with a tuft of gray hair and a pair of coveralls on. He was lighting a cigarette, his ear turned toward the radio.

All Jennifer could make out from the radio was the tinny sound of a large crowd hooting and clapping, almost drowning out the man who was speaking excitedly.

The men all turned and looked at her as the door closed. The two customers nodded at her, and the gray-haired man exhaled some smoke and gave her a tobacco-stained smile.

"Howdy, miss," he said.

"Hi. May I have the key to the ladies' room?"

"Yes, ma'am you can," he answered. He reached behind him, where several sets of keys hung. He removed one that had a block of wood with *Girls* written on it in black marker.

"Thank you."

Right outside and around the right," he said as he went back to his radio.

Jennifer took the key and walked back outside. The skinny guy was washing three-hundred miles of dirt from her windshield. She walked around the side of the building and opened the door with a woman's figure on it.

She used the restroom, then ran the water in the white sink until it was cool. She held her hands underneath it and patted her throat, the back of her neck, her face. She looked up and frowned at her reflection. She hadn't slept much the night before, too nervous to relax, and she'd left New Orleans early. She looked as tired as she felt. Her green eyes were marked with little twigs of red, and her face looked pale despite her tan. She tried not to feel sorry for herself.

Her warm, blonde hair was a mess, and the underside uncomfortably hot and wet against her neck. She pulled the big barrette out, pulled her hair into a ponytail as best she could, and clipped it up in back, letting the ponytail flop over. Her hair grew well past her shoulders, and it still touched her neck, but at least it wasn't hanging all over her.

She reached into her shirt and tugged at her bra straps, then dried her hands, threw the towel away, and went back outside. The bathroom had been dark, and she'd left her sunglasses on the passenger seat. The June glare singed her retinas, and she looked down at the sidewalk as she walked back inside.

She opened the door again, and the whooping and hollering of the men inside drowned out the little bell.

"I told you, Ben!" one of the men shouted. He held out his hand. "Gimme my dollar!"

"Aw, George, I only got a dollar-fifty on me," the other man said as he pulled out his billfold.

"Then you got enough to stop for a beer on your way home," George said, laughing.

Jennifer put the key by the cash register, then slid open the glass cooler in front of the counter.

"Told you not to take that bet, Ben" the man behind the counter said. "Everybody but you knew Secretariat was gonna take it."

"Everybody did not," Ben said, handing George some change. "Twenty-five years! Ah, who cares, anyhow? I'll stick with baseball, fellas."

When Jennifer straightened, the man behind the counter was headed her way, and the door opened behind her. She looked over her shoulder to see the skinny guy from outside.

He smiled broadly. "You're all set, miss. I topped off your water for ya."

"Thanks."

"What does she got, Ned?" the man at the register asked as he rang up her can of RC.

"Four-fifteen," Ned answered.

"Four-forty-seven," the man told Jennifer.

She reached into a zippered pocket in her purse, pulled out a five, and handed it to him.

"Keep the change," she said.

"Thank you, ma'am," the skinny guy said as he walked past her. "I heard y'all hollerin' all the way out there. Is it over?"

"George took my dollar," Ben said.

"Again?"

"Thank you," she said to the man behind the counter, who just nodded.

She stepped back out into the relentless heat. The clouds were building and darkening further east, and she hoped that she'd get underneath them before the rain was over. In summer, it rained every day around three, for about ten minutes. Unless there was a storm. Every Floridian knew that, too.

She slid back into the car and, when her hand brushed the scorching red leather seat, she was grateful she'd worn jeans instead of shorts. She cranked the engine and stuck her soda between her knees before pulling back out onto US 90.

The station she'd had on back near Pensacola was long gone. She reached over and punched at the buttons, past a gospel station, some news, and then a country and western station. Finally, she found a station playing Tony Orlando & Dawn. She was ready to cut the yellow ribbon into a hundred pieces, but she left it.

She felt her heart skip just a bit, from a mixture of excitement and dread. She hadn't been back in eleven years. She'd be there in less than an hour. Suddenly, she felt more like an eighteen-year-old girl than a thirty-year-old woman, and she had been one scared and broken teenager.

She tried to distract herself with the radio. Sang along to "Drift Away." Tried not to scream when "Bad, Bad Leroy Brown" came on. She had nothing against Jim Croce, but she'd heard it at least twenty times since Mobile.

She finally shut the radio off altogether, and let the silence be her company for the rest of the drive. She had just finished the last of her warm Tab when she rounded a bend in the road and saw it.

The sign was exactly the same as it had been when she'd left, except they'd adjusted the population a bit and touched up the orange blossom.

Welcome to Dismal, Florida! Population 6,028, at least one of whom murdered your family! Have a nice day!

CHAPTER 2

As she drove through the town, she looked around her like a tourist. It was so different, and yet so much the same. There were a few more filling stations, and the Food Fair her mother and grandmother had shopped in was now a Pantry Pride. There was a brand-new Zayre store at the other end of the Southland Shopping Center. The five and dime downtown, near the library, had been turned into a Woolworth's. The McDonald's was still there, and the Dairy Queen. Both of them made her shudder with memories suddenly too fresh and too plentiful.

Bob's Drive-Inn was an A & W, and it was doing a brisk business on this sweltering day. There was a new junior high school that would have looked huge when she was in sixth grade, but now it looked like a miniature version of the ones back in New Orleans.

She intentionally, with some trial and error, avoided Summer Street, and Palmetto High School. She drove past a couple of housing developments that hadn't been there in 1962, and the other shopping center, on the older, poorer side of town, where the Kash n' Karry was still holding up one end, Ace Hardware the other, and McCrory's was still squatting in the middle.

It only took five minutes to drive from the west side of town to the east. It had freshened up in some spots, declined in others, but it didn't seem all that much bigger than it had been. Jennifer was about to head on out Main Street, which would turn into Citrus Trail, which would lead to where she was going, but she pulled into the parking lot of a Rexall Drugs instead.

She didn't want to be in town. She didn't want to see anyone that knew her, and she was feeling a little shell-shocked, but she wasn't sure she was ready to go to the old homeplace, either. She also knew she'd need a few things, so she turned back onto the street and headed west again, back through town.

She pulled into a parking space at the Pantry Pride, and sat there a minute, listening to the rattle of shopping carts and the ticking of her engine. The last time she'd been here, she'd been with her mother. She'd never come back. She hoped it had been completely redone.

She got out of the car and took a deep breath before heading for the store.

A young man with shaggy brown hair and a walrus mustache was leaning against his hood, smoking a cigarette and listening to Cat Stevens on his car radio. A plump redheaded woman about Jennifer's age was loading her bags into the back of a fairly-new Gremlin. A toddler of indeterminate gender nibbled a cookie in the seat of the cart.

Jennifer hurried into the store, grateful for the cool air that met her, and grabbed a cart. She didn't want to be there long enough to run into anyone that might recognize her, so she scurried through the store, grabbing things as she saw them. Milk, coffee, sugar, orange juice. Some Grape-Nuts. A box of Space Food Sticks—peanut butter—her secret indulgence. She grabbed a six-pack of RC, bread and peanut butter, some fruit, and a few things like toilet paper and dish soap, and then headed for the register.

She thought she looked very different from the girl she was at eighteen. But she was also afraid that she really didn't, and that someone would suddenly call out her name, or worse, look at her the way they had right before she'd left. So, she pulled her sunglasses back down off her head and peered at the papers and magazines.

Lots of headlines and stories about Watergate, as usual. Jennifer wondered if the movie stars were ever going to stay in that place again, or if they were so sick of hearing the name that they didn't want to call for a reservation. Gas prices. Gas lines. She had enough problems; so she focused on the magazine covers instead. Robert Redford. Twelve dinners for twelve dollars. Sonny and Cher. How to decorate your room for under fifty dollars. Nice topics. Nothing sad, nothing scary.

When she'd first become a police officer for the city of New Orleans, she'd read every line of every paper, every day. Even though she'd spent two years as a meter maid and two as a dispatcher, she'd thought that keeping up with crime and other events would serve her as a cop. Two years ago, in her fifth year as an officer, she'd finally been allowed out onto the street. Within six months, she'd stopped reading the news. She saw enough of it.

She checked out without any problems and hurried to the car. She got a paper cut from the edge of one of her grocery bags, and she sucked her finger for a moment. She loaded the last of three bags and was about to get in when she saw the pay phone by the front door. She thought about that for a minute. She'd promised, and it was the right thing to do.

She shut her door again, and rummaged in her purse for the change she'd just been dumping in it all day. Very unlike her, with her need for everything to be where and as it should be. She finally pulled out a dime just as she reached the phone.

She was about to pull out the phone book when she realized that she still remembered the number. He answered it himself, on the third ring.

"Yeah!" he answered, cheerful and robust.

"Hi, Uncle Ray."

He didn't respond for a moment. She heard kids yelling at each other in the background. A television going.

"Well, hey, there, Jennifer Marie. Are you here?"

It threw her, the Marie. She hadn't heard it in a long time. "Yes, I just got to town."

"Where are ya?" She heard him put his hand loosely over the mouthpiece. "Would you kids please do that outside? I'm on the phone." He took his hand away. "Where are you, hon?"

"I just stopped to get a few things at Food Fair," she answered.

"It's a Pantry Pride now," he said. "Publix still isn't interested." He chuckled, and she smiled to be polite, even though he couldn't see it. "Well, we were expecting you tomorrow sometime, so Peggy hasn't had a chance to put a few things in the fridge over there. We did get the electricity back on yesterday, though."

"Thanks, I appreciate that," she said. "I'll pay you back when I see you."

"Don't worry about it, it's coming on your first bill. Electric company always gets theirs. Well, listen, why don't you come over for supper in a while?"

"Oh, thanks, that sounds nice, but could we do it tomorrow as planned? I'm pretty beat, and I'm sure I'll have a lot to do."

"Yeah, sure. That's fine." He paused for a bit and she was about to say goodbye when he spoke first. "I haven't...uh…told anybody. You know, besides Peggy. The job, of course. But I mean anyone else. You know."

"Okay." A few faces drifted into Jennifer's vision and she blinked them away. "I really appreciate everything you've done."

"Family's family," he said simply. "As far as the job, well, somebody was gonna have to fill it. Might as well be you, since you were coming anyway."

"Well, thanks for everything. I'd better go, before my stuff melts," she said, even though she hadn't bought anything frozen.

"Did you call the phone company?"

“No. I will in a day or so.” She didn’t mention that she didn’t really want the phone on just yet. Not that anyone would call her, but anyone who did would be uncomfortable to talk to.

“Okay, sure. But listen, are you sure you want to stay out there? I mean, right away? You’re welcome to stay in our guest room as long as you want.”

“I know. But, no. It was always my favorite place to be.”

“Okay, well. You need anything, you call us. Peggy and I both, we’re really glad you’re here.”

Jennifer wasn’t sure how true that was, but when she hung up the phone, she felt a little less alone.

CHAPTER 3

Once she'd gone a few miles out Citrus Trail she passed Orange Blossom Farms. They had a large grove, and in the respective seasons, they offered U-pick oranges, watermelons and strawberries. The farm stand where they sold to passersby was still on the side of the road near the entrance, though they'd added on to it and painted it white. After that, there was nothing for three miles, until her turn.

She knew it was coming, but it startled her anyway. She'd grown up there, and still knew every inch of it. She'd gone back there in her head many times while lying awake in bed. And yet, seeing it now was like seeing it in a movie somehow. Not real, but pretty close.

The mailbox was still at the road, still leaned, and was still painted a bright blue. She turned onto the dirt drive, leaving the mailbox behind her, and kept her eyes on the road in front of her, not looking up until she got to the end of the driveway. When she stopped the car, she stopped breathing, too.

It wasn't exactly as it had remained in her memory. There were no begonias underneath the huge old live oak that loomed over the roof in front, and there were no kalanchoe planted around the three smaller live oaks in the side yard. The birdbath that had been by the path to the front porch was gone. The old Nash Rambler wasn't in the driveway. The house and outbuildings had never been painted, but the wood looked lighter than she remembered, grayer.

The old place had been built in 1910, and from the outside, a visitor could almost imagine they'd gone back in time. The old wood frame and rough-cut timber house was the closest structure to the driveway, and shaped in an ell, with the ell pointing south. The tin roof was rust-colored, primarily, and there was a brick chimney on the south end of the house as well as the west.

The darker wood of the ell marked it as the addition it had been, back in 1938. Grandma and Grandpa had added a third bedroom and an inside bathroom that year, when Jennifer's mother had been thirteen, and Grandpa had thought it best that she not share a room anymore with her younger brother, James. James was gone, now, too, killed in Korea three days after he'd gotten there.

This had been Jennifer's wonderland, her safe haven, her yellow brick road. She and her brother had much preferred the freedom of Grandma's acreage to the little house in town that they'd shared with their father.

As kids, she, Jonah, and their friends had taken apples and carrots to the old work horse, Roosevelt, that had lived out his days in the pasture behind the small, log stable. They'd picked strawberries from Grandma's beds behind the old outhouse, where Grandma had said they grew best. They'd dragged the hose over to the garden rows and watered the lettuce and the tomatoes and their hot, tanned legs. They'd climbed the orange tree behind the shed and picked the brown-speckled fruits, which would be the sweetest. Then they'd thrown the peels at each other as the juice ran down their chests and they swatted the bees away.

Jennifer sat in the quiet car, staring out the windshield at the place that had meant everything to her, and to Grandma and Mom and Jonah.

Now there was just Jennifer, if you didn't count her drunken and broken father, and she did not.

She hadn't brought much; her 13-inch television, a couple suitcases of clothes and linens, a box of books. A few necessities, like her radio, her alarm clock, her blow dryer and her potted philodendron. It only took her ten minutes to bring it all inside from the car.

Then she sat down at the Formica kitchen table, in the yellow-flowered chair she'd sat in whenever she'd eaten in Grandma's kitchen.

She looked around her, and let the memories wash over her, let herself be surprised by little details she'd forgotten.

It had been three months since Grandma had passed. Jennifer had been on her first vacation as an adult, in Puerto Rico. In any case, she had moved since she'd last spoken to Grandma, two weeks before her death, and Uncle Ray couldn't find her new address in Grandma's red leather address book. The letter was finally forwarded to the efficiency she'd rented three weeks after Grandma's death. A peaceful death, unexpected, in her sleep. Jennifer should have called when she'd gotten back to New Orleans. She'd meant to, and there was a packet of photos in her purse, with copies that were intended for Grandma.

There had been no memorial to miss; Anna Mae Quindlen had wanted nothing of the kind.

Words had been said before the Sunday service at Orangewood Methodist Church, where Grandma, her friends, and Uncle Ray attended. Her ashes had been scattered underneath the live oak out front.

Uncle Ray had said they'd left almost everything in the house, except for those things she had willed to certain friends or family. Grandma had wanted her clothes donated to the Salvation Army, and her books had been left to the library. Her good china went to her best friend's daughter, Tricia. Everything else, she'd left to Jennifer.

Grandma had told her to go far away and never to come back, though they had discussed visiting over the last couple of years. Jennifer had trouble understanding why she would have left her the house, and the thirty-two acres on which it sat. Maybe so she could make her own decision about whether to come back.

The same old Lady Kenmore refrigerator hummed in one corner, but it wasn't as big as she'd remembered. There was a clock in the shape of a barn that hadn't been there before, but the hunk of Formica that had been missing from the end of the counter was still gone.

Almost everything she saw, Jennifer had a memory to go with it. She let them drift around the room for a bit, then remembered that she had groceries to put away. Her few things looked sparse in the old fridge, but it was enough for now, and the fridge was cold. The rest of the things, she put in the same cupboards they would have gone in ten, fifteen, twenty-five years ago.

When she was done, she found some aluminum ice trays in the freezer and filled them. Then she went around the house, opening all of the original windows. The ceilings in the house were high, and the windows narrow and tall. She opened them all, propping the one in her mother's old room, which still needed propping. She had just opened the last one when she suddenly smelled iron, and the skies opened up.

The rain didn't ease its way in, it was just suddenly and completely there. It pounded on the metal roof, and Jennifer grabbed an apple and went out through the kitchen door and onto the back porch.

The chairs and Grandma's rocker were neatly piled on top of each other at one end of the porch, and Jennifer didn't feel like putting them right, so she sat down on the top step and took a bite of her apple. The huge garden was now just a rectangle of dirt dotted with dandelions and stickers, but the old tire swing still hung from the tree in front of the shed. Grandma had said a few times, over the past few years, that gardening in the heat had started to wear her out too fast.

The rain cooled the breeze just enough for it to feel good, and the smell of good, wet earth made Jennifer's nose twitch. As the breeze picked up, the tire swing moved just a hair.

"You remember the time you filled that tire swing with water and tried to raise tadpoles in it?" Grandma asked.

Jennifer looked over her shoulder and smiled. Grandma was sitting in her red rocker, pinching the tips off a strainer full of green beans. She looked like she had when Jennifer was about twelve or thirteen. Her silver hair was pinned back low on her neck, and over one ear was the enamel hairpin Jennifer had bought her from McCrory's, the one with the daisies on it. She was wearing the red gingham apron with the rick-rack around the pocket.

"I remember," Jennifer said. "You didn't care how much I cried and stomped; you made me cart every one of those things back to the creek."

Grandma laughed softly. "Not all of them. Some of them you didn't get."

"I know," Jennifer said. "We couldn't swing in that old tire for weeks."

"You were so mad at me," Grandma said, smiling. She had a short bean in her hand, and she popped it into her mouth. "Too small."

"Not really," Jennifer said. "I just felt bad because some of them died, just like you told me they would."

"Well, some of the tadpoles died, but plenty of them grew up safe and sound," Grandma said. "God knew how many frogs He needed in the world that summer."

Jennifer nodded and took a bite of her apple. It stuck a bit in her suddenly dry throat, as she wondered why God had needed one less mother, one less brother and one less friend, in the fall of 1962.

"Why don't you go on in and wash up, Jennifer Marie," Grandma said. "You're all muddy from picking these beans."

"Okay." Jennifer looked out toward the woods in back of the yard. "I miss you."

"I miss you, too."

Jennifer felt her eyes water, and she blinked a few times, then stood up and stretched her back. Her eyes glanced over the old red rocker in the corner, underneath a couple of wooden chairs, before she walked back into the kitchen and let the screen door shut behind her.

CHAPTER 4

It rained off and on for most of the night.

Jennifer put her things away in her mother's old room. When her mother left her father, they'd come to live with Grandma. Jennifer had been given her mother's room, and Claire had roomed with Grandma. The white eyelet curtains were still there, and the white wrought iron bed that had belonged to her mom. Jennifer found a few cardboard boxes and shoeboxes in the floor of the tall, narrow closet; they were filled with books, mementos and photographs that had been in this room when Jennifer had left. She was tempted to sit down and go through them, but she put her clothes away instead, and made up her bed.

Her box of books and records she left in a corner of the small living room. Grandma's television set was gone, and Jennifer set hers up on a small table across from the flowered couch. She spent several minutes fiddling with the antennae, and finally managed to get three of the four channels that she knew about, and left it on just for the company.

She only half-listened to *All in the Family* as she set up her stereo on the tea cart that Grandma had used for her houseplants, which were gone. As for her own plant, Jennifer ended up giving it a drink and then putting it on the kitchen table.

Once she was done, she couldn't help wandering around, touching things, remembering. Grandma's room looked almost exactly like it always had. The same eyelet curtains as in Jennifer's room. The same white linen runner across the pine dresser, the one with the whitework that Grandma had done when she'd gotten engaged.

There were a few boxes in Grandma's closet, too, one held objects wrapped in newspaper. Jennifer unwrapped one of the ones on top. It was the old picture, from the 1930s, of Grandma and Grandpa sitting on the back porch. Grandma's hair was jet black and worn pinned back. Grandpa was frozen eternally in the middle of a belly laugh, with the sunlight or overexposure turning his golden hair almost white.

On the grass by the porch steps, Jennifer's mother, Claire, was waving at the camera, her smile revealing one missing front tooth.

Jennifer swiped a little bit of dust from the glass, and set the picture back onto Grandma's empty-looking dresser, where she'd always kept it.

She glanced down at the rest of the boxes. The one on the bottom was marked "Photos" in red ink, written in Grandma's graceful hand. They used to go through that box sometimes, on rainy days, spreading the pictures around them on Grandma's bed. Jennifer was tempted to look at them now, but she knew that would be a rabbit hole. She folded the flaps on the box of breakables and closed the closet door.

After a quick shower in the old clawfoot tub, Jennifer decided she was hungry. She found one of the aluminum TV trays in the mud room, and she took it with her into the living room. She ate a late dinner of peanut butter and jelly and a glass of Ovaltine, watching *Mission: Impossible.* She missed most of it. The rain hammering the tin roof made it hard to hear, but she didn't feel like getting up to raise the volume. She ended up turning it off before it was over, and went to bed.

"What time does Daniel get off work?" Inez asked.

Jennifer looked up at her as she struggled to shove her wet foot into her sneaker. "He said eight-thirty."

Inez smoothed her shiny, chin-length, black hair, which either she or Mama Tyne usually ironed. Inez's skin was a smooth, beautiful, light-brown, her eyes almost exotic in their almond shape. She smiled widely over at Jennifer.

"Well, we don't want to get you back late, do we? You guys have been apart a whole day," she said, teasing.

"Quit it," Jennifer said, grinning. "You and Jonah are just as bad."

"Now, you know that's not true. We don't get to spend half the time together that you two do."

Both of the girls' smiles dimmed a bit.

"Well. One day," Jennifer said. She purposely brightened. "But today was great, right?"

Inez smiled back, as she buckled the thin blue belt around the waist of her light green shirtdress. "It was. I wish we could go to the drive-in with you, though."

"So do I." Jennifer got her other shoe on, and picked up her wet bathing suit from a nearby rock. Hers was navy blue, with white polka dots. Next to it was Inez's suit, the green one she'd ordered from Montgomery Ward back in the summer. It was hard to believe it was October already. Pretty soon it would be too cool for swimming in the lake.

Inez finished buckling her sandals, and straightened up. At 5'7, she was just an inch taller than Jennifer, but she always seemed taller. Maybe it was the long legs, or her unforced dignity.

A horn blew back over by the lake. Both girls turned to look, even though several hundred feet of woods kept them from being able to see Ned's Galaxie.

"The boys are getting impatient," Jennifer said. "Probably getting eaten up alive."

"Jonah's not impatient; he's still dead to the world. We're gonna have to sit up front with Ned."

They started walking along the pine needle-covered path, back toward the car. "I told him he was getting too much sun," Jennifer said.

Inez knuckled Jennifer in the shoulder. "'You're my twin sister, not my mom'," she parodied, dropping her voice a couple registers.

"You can have him," Jennifer said.

"I do." Inez laughed.

"Oh, hold on," Jennifer said. "I need to pee."

"Can't you hold it?" her best friend asked, slapping at her shin.

"No. Too much soda." Jennifer waved her on. "I'll hurry. Tell them I'll be right there."

"Okay, but be quick," Inez said, continuing along the path.

Sudden panic made Jennifer's heart pound, and she knew she was dreaming. She hadn't panicked then.

"Inez, wait!" she yelled in her dream, but Inez was gone from the path.

For whatever reason, because dreams sometimes don't make sense, Jennifer went ahead and squatted by a tree, pulling down her panties and lifting her yellow sundress. She had just finished patting herself dry with her handkerchief when the shots rang out. Three. Four. Six.

Suddenly, Jennifer was already back by the lake, staring at Ned's father's 1959 Galaxie. Jennifer heard the roar of an engine, and tires on gravel, but this time she didn't look up to see the taillights disappearing around the bend, or hear the whoops and hollers of the men who were driving it.

First, she saw the back of Ned's head, leaning against the window frame. Blood that made no sense in Jennifer's world was running down the side of the driver's door. Then she realized that Inez was yelling over the car radio, which Ned had been blasting. That week's hottest song, "The Locomotion", which seemed so inappropriate, already.

"Jonah!" Inez was screaming, as she scrambled from the front passenger seat to the back.

Jennifer ran to the driver's side and yanked open the back door. Inez was on all fours over Jonah, who was lying on his side. His eyes were wide open, his cheeks a flaming, painful-looking pink. There was blood on the back of his neck, and on the seat beneath him. Blood dripped, too, from Inez's shoulder onto the side of Jonah's white T-shirt.

"No," Jennifer said. "No," she kept saying. She was almost grunting the word. The sound reminded some part of her brain of a mama bear, warning away some danger.

She dropped to her knees, barely feeling the gravel cutting into her skin.

Jonah's eyes were wide open, and for the first time in her life, Jennifer could not feel some part of her twin living inside her.

Struggling to awaken, 1973 Jennifer felt a terrible sadness for 1962 Jennifer. She wanted to warn her somehow, prepare her for the fact that in just two weeks, her mother would be dead, too.

She sat straight up in bed, panting for air, the front of her thin T-shirt sticky with sweat, tears streaming down her cheeks.

"Jonah?" she managed to croak.

But he was never there.

CHAPTER 5

Grandma had kept a clean house, even up into her eighties, but the place had been empty for a few months. Dust had collected and the damp had gotten in, so Jennifer spent most of the day cleaning. Then she'd had some lunch and gone out to the yard.

She didn't have any flowers to plant in the places where Grandma had liked to have flowers. She didn't have much in her savings, either. The flowers would have to wait until she got a few paychecks from the new job. So, she worked on the front porch instead.

She swept a pile of leaves, dust and debris into a dustpan, and dumped it into a paper bag, then checked her watch. It was after two. She was due at Uncle Ray's at six.

Uncle Ray wasn't blood; he'd been her mother Claire's best friend growing up. They'd even touched on the idea of dating, but once they'd gone to the junior prom together, they'd realized they were really just friends. They continued their friendship into adulthood, and it hadn't seemed to matter to Jennifer's father early in her parents' marriage. Later on, her father had used insecurity as part of his justification for his alcoholism. But then, he'd had plenty of other excuses, too.

Now Ray had grandchildren, and Jennifer's mother never would.

It had been good of Ray to offer her the job. Female cops weren't as popular in Dismal, FL as they were in New Orleans, and they weren't all that well-liked in New Orleans. The fact that Uncle Ray had hired her was going to anger most of the other officers. Maybe all of them. Not only was she a female, she was also practically family.

She went inside and grabbed a rag and some vinegar to wipe down the old chairs and the swing, which she'd found in the shed and rehung. When she came back out, she heard a car coming up the drive. When it rounded the bend in the drive, she saw it was a pickup, light blue, with a white roof and a white strip around the bottom. A Chevrolet, she thought.

She didn't know what Uncle Ray drove, but she stopped thinking that mattered after the truck stopped behind her car. It was the shape of the face, the jawline, which was in partial profile. The glint of the sun off short, ash-blonde hair.

She stood there at the porch rail, frozen. He waited in the truck for what felt like forever then, all of a sudden, he jerked the door open and got out.

She watched him as he walked across the driveway and started up the path to the house.

He'd been really handsome in high school, but he was even more so now. His hairline was just a bit higher, but he was still as trim as he'd ever been. A bit more muscular, perhaps. He was wearing faded jeans that were not bellbottoms, and a red plaid shirt with the tails out. When he stopped about ten feet shy of the porch and looked her in the face, she saw that his eyes were still just as blue. He had about two days' growth on his face, which she knew from memory only took him one day to grow.

She had to remember to take a breath before she finally spoke. "Hi," she said quietly.

He shoved his hands in his front pockets. "Hi." His tone was curt.

They stared at each other just long enough for her to really need something to say. "You look good."

"So do you," he said, after a moment.

She was standing there in her bare, dirty feet. Her hair was piled on top of her head, held there mainly by cobwebs, and her shorts and T-shirt were covered with dirt and dust. She looked like Carol Burnett's janitor lady, and she knew it.

"How did you know I was here?" she asked him.

"My cousin Cindy's the manager at Pantry Pride."

There was no warmth at all in his voice, not that she'd expected any. Maybe. But not with any real hope.

"Well, that figures," she said. "I've been to one place in town, and it would have to be someplace where somebody in your family worked."

"Why?" He raised his eyebrows. "Are you hiding out?"

"No. I just…I was just getting settled in before I saw anybody."

"Like me?" he asked shortly.

"What do you mean?" she asked, afraid of the answer.

"Were you going to see me?"

"Of course. I would have to, eventually." Her voice wound down. "Of course."

They stared at each other for a minute.

"Do you want to come in?" she asked.

"No." He was pretty matter-of-fact about that. "In fact, this was a mistake."

He turned and took a few steps, then spun back around, pointing at her.

"Not one phone call!" he snapped. "Not even one!"

"I'm sorry," she said. She had no defense for that.

He took a couple of steps closer and put his hands on his hips. "I went looking for you in Fort Lauderdale, did you know that?"

That punched her in the chest. She swallowed. "No. I didn't know that."

"I thought maybe since we talked about going there for our honeymoon, maybe you were there. If you were, I didn't find you."

"I was in New Orleans," she replied quietly.

"That's nice," he said, nodding. "I looked for you in Fort Lauderdale for two months."

"I'm sorry," she said again.

"Screw you," he said back.

He turned and started walking away again. She wanted him to go. She wanted him to stay. He didn't seem to know, either, because he turned back around again.

"I *begged* you to stay!"

"I couldn't!"

"I know you were scared!" He was yelling now. "I knew you might be in danger, but I would have taken care of you!"

"You were just a kid, Daniel," she replied. "I was just a kid!"

"You would have been okay," he snapped. "I would have made sure of it!"

Jennifer swallowed, and felt her eyes heat up. She'd always cried so easily; at romantic movies, sad books, roadkill, even sappy commercials. He might have forgotten that. The last thing she needed was to cry in front of him now.

He came a little closer to the porch. He was still a good ten feet away, but she couldn't help studying his face, remembering in better detail all of the features she thought she'd remembered perfectly.

"I knew you were scared," he said again, toning it down. "I told you if you had to leave, I would go with you, and you were just *gone*."

"Daniel, you still needed to finish your senior year—"

"So did you!"

"I did!"

He looked like he was biting something back. He put his hands on his hips and looked down at the path. She had forgotten how she used to think he looked a little like Paul Newman.

"Why are you here? She died months ago," he said to his feet.

"Three months ago."

"Whatever."

"I wanted…I wanted to see…everything again," she said. "And I want to know what happened."

She didn't need to tell him what she meant. He jerked his head up.

"Nobody knows, Jen! Nobody knew then and nobody knows now."

"Somebody knows," she said firmly.

"So why not hire a detective or something? Because as far as the police are concerned, it's a dead end. It was a dead end eleven years ago."

"I want to see for myself. That's one of the reasons I—"

"So hire a PI! You could have done that from New Orleans!"

He turned around yet again, and started walking away, yet again.

She had also forgotten how he interrupted her when he was mad, and how much that pissed her off.

"Well, I didn't!" she snapped. "I apologize for ruining your life by coming back here to do it!"

He stopped and turned around. "No, lady," he snapped, pointing at the ground, "This is not how you ruined my life."

He started for the driveway again.

"Daniel, wait!" she called. "I need to talk to you about—"

"Should have done that eleven years ago," he said without turning.

"Please," she called.

He waved her off. She watched him yank his door open and climb into his truck. He didn't look her way again. His tires ground at the rocks and dirt as he turned the truck around and sped back down the driveway.

Jennifer felt like she'd been hollowed out with a grapefruit spoon. What had eventually become a dull ache was now a raw, inflamed wound. He'd been the very best part of her life, the most important thing. She would have followed him anywhere, done anything for him. Anything but stay. She bit her lip and blinked her eyes, refusing to give in to tears. If *that* floodgate ever opened again, she'd be useless to herself.

She stood there watching until most of the dust had settled back down on the ground. Then she turned around and pulled the screen door open. She stubbed her big toe horrifically on the threshold and gave herself something else to be upset about. As she stood there on one foot, the other one dripping blood all over the porch floor, she was exceptionally grateful for that.

"Why, you kids are always having such spats," Grandma said.

"Yeah," Jennifer managed.

She looked over her shoulder. Grandma was sitting on the swing, an embroidery basket by her feet, the hoop in her lap. It was the sampler that had been hanging on the bathroom wall since Jennifer was in tenth grade. Jennifer had hung it herself.

"He doesn't understand," she said, wiping at her toe with the rag.

"Of course, he doesn't understand," Grandma said. "He's a hurt, angry young man. But he loves you so much. He'll come around, like he always does."

Grandma could have been talking about the fight they'd had right before prom, or the time Daniel had seen Tommy Weathers kiss her behind the concession stand, or the time she'd broken up with Daniel for three days because somebody told her he'd been seeing Liz Ballard on the side. It had been a lie. Come to think of it, Grandma had been wearing that same blue dress for that one.

"Go get a Band-Aid and some sweet tea. Eventually, he'll call," Grandma said. "But please do not stretch that cord all the way into the laundry room. I am not eavesdropping."

"Well, not anymore," Jennifer mumbled. She hopped over to the swing, grabbed her dustpan and trash bag, and hopped back into the house.

Daniel turned onto Citrus Trail from Jennifer's driveway and went about twenty feet before he slammed on the brakes, only thinking to look in his rear-view after the fact.

Both hands gripping the wheel, he leaned forward and blew out a breath. He should go back. He should go back and yell at her some more. He should go back and tell her what a child she had been, how thoughtless and cruel. He should go back and grab onto her and tell her he understood, and that it was okay now.

But it wasn't okay. He did understand, but that didn't make it okay. It didn't make him okay.

He shouldn't have come here. He shouldn't have come here ten minutes after hearing she was back. He should have taken some time to think about it, to sort it out. Instead, he'd come flying over here to see her, all twisted up with anger and hurt and wonder and gratitude and pride and righteous indignation. All of that. More.

"Damn it," he said quietly, tapping his forehead against the wheel. "Damn it."

A horn blew behind him and he jerked upright and looked in the rear-view. Old Tom Woods, in his old Ford truck.

Daniel stuck a hand out the window and stepped on the gas.

Uncle Ray had moved from the little brown house on Elmwood to a newer house over on Patterson. It was a nice house; simple, but nice. The front yard was neatly trimmed, and they had two cars; Ray drove a green, four-year-old Riviera, and Peggy an almost new brown Buick Estate Wagon.

There was a nice patio with a barbecue grill in the back, and the big back yard was definitely geared for the grandkids, with a trampoline, a tetherball pole, and a sandbox. Somebody's bright green Inchworm was sitting next to a red hibiscus, waiting for its next rider.

Jennifer, Ray, Peggy, and their family were squeezed into a modest dining room. Their daughter Carrie, who was about five years younger than Jennifer, was there with her husband Paul, a dark-haired man in black-rimmed glasses, whom Carrie had met at Florida State. Between them were their three kids, Annie, Jason and Rickie, five, four and two respectively.

Jennifer had lived with just her Great-Aunt Milly in New Orleans, then with a roommate, and then alone. Now, she'd been alone at Grandma's out in the country for two days. The boisterous cacophony of this animated family was almost a shock to her system, but she envied it all the same.

Uncle Ray was as handsome as Jennifer remembered, tall and thin, with neatly-cut dark brown hair that was going gray around the ears. It matched the mustache, which seemed to have turned gray all at once.

Aunt Peggy was still a pretty woman, a bit heavier than she'd been a dozen years before, but with her blond hair done in a flip and her smooth skin, she made a lovely grandmother. Carrie was her spitting image. Jennifer and Carrie had never been especially close because of their age difference. They mostly saw each other at family get-togethers. The last time Jennifer had seen her, she was wearing her band uniform, twirling a baton in their old front yard. Jennifer wondered where *her* baton had gone. She'd twirled just for fun, but she'd enjoyed it.

"I'm sorry, what?" she asked Peggy.

"I asked if you were excited about starting your new job," Peggy said with a warm smile.

"Oh. Yes, I suppose so," Jennifer answered. She looked at Uncle Ray. "I mean, of course I am. I'm just still getting used to being here."

"You're gonna do just fine, hon," Ray said. "Carrie, baby, pass me those potatoes, please. You'll be fine,

Jennifer. I think once the guys get used to you—not just because you're our first female officer—but because you're new, I think we'll be pretty glad you're here."

Carrie passed the potatoes, then leaned over her plate. "Jennifer, have you talked to *Daniel* yet?"

She whispered Daniel's name, like nobody would hear her, or know who he was, anyway.

"Actually, yeah," Jennifer answered, her stomach churning as she remembered his angry face. "He came by the house today."

"Oh!" Carrie said.

"How'd that go?" Uncle Ray asked. Before she could answer, his attention was captured by something Jason was doing down at the end of the table.

"About as badly as I expected," Jennifer answered, pushing a carrot around on her plate. "I'm pretty sure—"

"Jason?" Carrie's husband asked.

Carrie jumped up. "Daddy, he's choking!"

Uncle Ray was coming out of his seat already, and Jennifer and Peggy stood as he rushed down the table. He pulled Jason out of his chair and whomped him a few times on the back. As his mother ran around the table, Jason coughed out a chunk of dinner roll, which flew across the table and landed on his mother's plate.

Jennifer stood there as everyone heaved their sighs of relief, offered him some water, and admonished him to chew his food better. Once everything settled, and everyone was back in their chairs, conversation turned to Watergate, unfortunately.

CHAPTER 6

Two days later, Jennifer sat on the guest side of Ray's big, scarred, oak desk, filling out a pile of paperwork with the black, almost useless, pen that came in a little wooden stand with his name on it.

She'd been there for almost an hour, and they were still working on it. Insurance, benefits, policies, attendance and sick days, tax forms, and so on. She'd already been fingerprinted and photographed, taken her uniform out to her car, and allowed Ray to inspect her Smith & Wesson Chiefs Special. It wasn't uncommon for departments to prefer officers provide their own weapons; they felt it ensured proper maintenance and care. Back in New Orleans, most officers favored the .357 Magnum or Colt's Police and Trooper model, but the Chiefs Special was one of the lighter and more compact double-action revolvers, and better fit Jennifer's smaller hand. The three other female officers Jennifer knew in New Orleans had preferred it, as well.

"Here you, go," Ray said as he walked back into the office with a paper cup of coffee in his hand.

"Oh, thanks, Ray," Jennifer said. She took the cup from him and he walked around his desk.

"Almost six. Day shift's gonna start coming in to close out the day's business, and night shift's starting to straggle in." He sat down heavily, and though he was more height than breadth, his well-worn leather chair protested. "Everybody knows we're gonna meet here for a few minutes before the evening muster."

Jennifer swallowed. She wasn't looking forward to seeing Daniel, who she knew was working day shift this month. Ray might be Daniel's boss, but he'd sort of been family, too, by association, and Ray had said they were still pretty close. Jennifer knew they would have discussed her this morning, talked about their first meeting after eleven years. She'd been afraid to ask Ray how that went. She was scared he'd tell her things she didn't really want to hear.

As Jennifer drank her coffee and hurried up with the forms, she could hear more and more activity and conversation on the other side of Ray's door.

Without meaning to, she kept trying to pick out Daniel's voice. She couldn't. Whether that was because he wasn't there, he wasn't talking, or she no longer had her Daniel radar, she didn't know.

Jennifer filled out the last form and handed the pile back to Ray. He called his assistant, Margo, in to make appropriate copies and file everything away, and let the officers know they'd be meeting in the bullpen in just a moment. After Margo had left, Jennifer drank her coffee down, clutched her folder of informational brochures and carbon copies to her chest, and Ray ushered her out of the office. They stopped just outside his door.

There were ten desks in the room, in five back-to-back pairs. There were fourteen officers in the room. As Ray got everyone's attention and voices died down, Jennifer looked around the room. There was only one officer she knew for sure, Pete Brandeis. He'd been one year behind them in high school. He looked about the same, with maybe just a little more of a paunch.

The only other familiar face was Daniel's and he was staring right at her.

"Okay, people, let's get this going, so you can get home or get to work," Ray said. "As you know, Title VII of the Civil Rights Act mandates that there will be no gender discrimination in public agencies, and we are a public agency."

Jennifer heard someone grumble, but she didn't want to look to see who it was. She kept her eyes on Ray.

"We are one of many departments in Florida that does not yet have a female officer," Ray continued. "The Governor wants that resolved. Our ladies in dispatch are civilians, they do not count. Now. This is Jennifer Sheehan. I know her and her family well, but she also comes well-recommended by the New Orleans Police Department."

There was more grumbling, a couple of sighs. A tall, redheaded cop spoke up. "What's the matter, she couldn't find a husband?"

"That's enough, Borman," Ray said.

"No offense, Chief, but girls don't have any business in police work," a blond cop said. "What about when she gets knocked up, or she's in a bad mood because she got her period?"

Jennifer had heard all of this before, many times, and it didn't really bother her anymore, but when she glanced over at Daniel, she felt her cheeks redden just a bit. He was clenching his jaw as he stared at his desk, but she was embarrassed for him to hear her roasted.

Ray held up a hand. "Let's keep the talk professional, guys. Or do it later at Monty's."

"Women still get their man-o-pause, or did they get liberated from that, too?" the blond cop asked the room, grinning. A few guys chuckled.

"Can it, Patterson," Daniel said quietly, to his desk. "She might be a cop, but she's still a lady."

"Uh oh," the redhead said, smiling. "The son of a preacher man has spoken."

The redheaded cop named Borman started singing, "Son of a Preacher Man."

Patterson and another guy joined in.

Jennifer felt like she'd been gut-shot. When she'd first heard that song back in '69, she'd cried for an hour. Even now, when she heard it, she ached.

"You're too late, guys," Brandeis spoke up. "That was back in high school. Wasn't it, Huddleston?"

There were a few "well, wells" and the like. Everybody looked at Daniel. Jennifer looked at the floor.

"Enough!" Ray yelled, and heads snapped around. "I've had enough. If you've got something smart to say, say it somewhere else. Officer Sheehan is not a rookie. She's spent her last two years with New Orleans on patrol. What I'm saying to you is that she is a qualified officer of the law. Am I understood?"

There were a few "Yeahs", a couple of "Yes, sirs." Most of them sounded reluctant.

"Messer, you're going to be her partner for the time being," Ray said. "Is that going to sit okay with you or do we need to discuss it?"

Jennifer turned to look at a slim, black-haired man who looked a few years older than her. He was leaning against his desk. She didn't recognize him.

"I don't have a problem with it," he said. He smiled at Jennifer. "You gotta pack a lunch, though, because my wife's expecting and we're saving up. I'm not going out for lunch every day, okay?"

Jennifer sort of returned his smile and cleared her throat. "That's cool with me."

"Geez, Messer, you tell everybody within five minutes that your wife's pregnant," a blond cop in the corner said.

"Why not? I'm proud of it."

"He just wants everybody to know he's got lead in his pencil," said a short, redheaded cop by the filing cabinets.

A few guys chuckled, and Messer smiled over his shoulder at the redhead. "I thought we established that when your son was born, Whitney."

That got a few genuine laughs. Jennifer glanced over at Daniel. He was staring at the pencil he was slowly tapping against his desk. She glanced around the room and caught Pete Brandeis's eye. Yeah, he remembered her.

"Any questions, gentlemen, or can we get on with our day?" Ray asked.

A gray-haired man who sat in the desk across from Daniel spoke up. "I don't have any questions…I just don't know how I feel about having lady police officers." He looked at Jennifer and shrugged.

"Well, Michaels, it's kind of a new thing," Ray said drolly, but with a bit of a smile.

"Maybe on *Mod Squad*," a tall, blond guy with a mustache grumbled.

Ray waved him off, then looked around the room. "Any actual questions?"

A few guys said "No" and others just shook their heads.

"Okay, then, Porter, take evening muster," Ray said to an older officer at the back. "Messer, Huddleston, would you join us inside for a minute, please?"

Daniel's head shot up. He looked around, then stood as some of the officers got their things together, and the rest followed Porter down the hall.

Jennifer heard one of the guys say, "Next thing you know, we'll be recruiting fags, too."

Ray jerked his head at Jennifer, and she preceded him into his office. Once Messer and Daniel were in, he closed the door. He walked over and leaned against his desk.

"Anthony, this is Jennifer. Jennifer, Anthony."

Anthony Messer leaned over and held out a hand. "Pleasure."

"Thank you," Jennifer said as they shook. "Same here."

He smiled at her. "Don't worry, most of those guys will come around." Jennifer just nodded. "You prefer Sheehan, Jennifer, Jenny, Jen, what?"

Only Daniel and Inez had called her Jen. And Jonah, but Jonah didn't call her anything anymore. She could see Daniel in her peripheral vision, but she was afraid to look at him.

"Jennifer's fine, or Sheehan," she answered. "Whichever."

"Jennifer's going to start with you in the morning," Ray said. "I know you'll do a good job of helping her settle in."

Messer shrugged. "Yeah, sure," he said.

"I'd like you to bring her up to date on that pot case you're working. Otherwise, just make sure she knows who's who and what's what in y'all's section, all right?"

"Yeah, Chief."

"Okay, we'll see you bright and early," Ray said.

"Yeah. See you tomorrow," Messer said to Jennifer. He glanced curiously at Daniel as he walked out of the office and shut the door behind him.

Ray stared at Daniel. Jennifer stared at Daniel. Daniel stared at the floor, hands on his hips. Jennifer couldn't help noticing that he looked great in the black uniform.

"Daniel?" Ray asked finally. Daniel looked at him and raised his eyebrows. "You need to say something?"

Daniel started to smile, then shook his head slightly. Then he looked back at the floor. "Well."

He huffed out a short laugh and looked up at them. "Well, this is nice."

Ray frowned at him.

"I would have appreciated a little warning," he said to Ray.

Ray looked at Jennifer. "I thought you said y'all talked yesterday."

"We sure as hell didn't talk about this," Daniel said, shaking his head.

"I tried to," she said to Ray. Then she looked over at Daniel, whose blue eyes were suddenly focused on her. "I was trying to tell you when you stormed off."

"You didn't try very hard, 'cause I would have stuck around to hear that."

Ray looked from Daniel to Jennifer and back again, then sighed. "You two need to go have a talk, somewhere besides here."

He pushed himself off the edge of his desk.

"That's okay," Daniel said. "Everything's fine."

He walked out of the office, leaving the door open behind him. Jennifer watched him walk through the bullpen toward the front door.

"I would have appreciated a little warning, too," Ray said.

"I'm sorry. I was starting to tell you when Jason started choking," she said.

"Jennifer, you were at the house for at least an hour after that."

She sighed, and nodded. "I know. I chickened out."

"With him or me?"

"I chickened out of telling you I chickened out with him," she said. "He did storm off, but I could have told him."

Ray sighed. "Well, my dear, I'm your boss and your family, not your therapist. Y'all are gonna have to figure it out from here. Just make sure it doesn't interfere with either one of y'all's jobs. Personal stuff gets cops hurt, so find a way to either work together or ignore each other."

"I understand."

Ray nodded. "All right. As for the rest of the guys, there are a couple of 'em that are pieces of work, but most of these men are good cops. Good people, too. The world's just changing too fast for 'em is all."

Jennifer smiled at him. "I'm sure it'll be fine once they get used to me."

Ray patted her shoulder. "Get out of here, hon. I've got stuff to do so I can go on home."

Jennifer was opening one of the glass front doors when she heard a door behind her. She looked over her shoulder and saw Daniel coming out of the men's room. He saw her, and headed toward the door, but didn't meet her eye.

She heard his hard-soled shoes on the asphalt behind her as she walked to her Dart. She hadn't locked it. She opened the back door, hissing as the metal door handle scorched her fingers, and dumped her purse and paperwork on the back seat.

When she looked up, Daniel was watching her over the roofs of the two cars between her Dart and his pick-up.

"You know, I used to imagine all the time…seeing you again. Where we'd be, what we'd say, how it would pan out." He shook his head. "This is not any of the ways I imagined it."

He opened his door and started to get in, then got back out. "How do you think it made me feel to have those jackasses talking about you like that?"

"How it made *you* feel? They were talking about *me*, not you."

He stared at her a moment. "Well, at one time that was the same thing," he said quietly.

Jennifer didn't know what she wanted to say, which was just as well, because he got in his truck and drove away.

CHAPTER 7

The phone company had hooked the phone back up that morning. Jennifer had been given a number that didn't match the one written on the yellow wall phone in Grandma's kitchen, and she felt like that was wrong somehow. She wasn't going to scratch the old one out.

She looked up Mama Tyne in the phone book Grandma kept in the drawer under the phone, with her S & H Green Stamp books and catalog. The Tynes still lived in the same house over on Milton Street, in what people used to call Colored Town. She didn't know what they called it now. They still had the phone number Jennifer had known most of her life.

Jennifer picked up the phone, but hesitated, so long that the dial tone stopped and that obnoxious beeping started. She pushed down the hook and the dial tone came back. She cleared her throat and got prepared, but hung up when the beeping started again.

She got herself an RC from the fridge, took a few swallows, then took a deep breath and dialed.

It was answered on the second ring. "Hello?"

Jennifer felt her throat tighten, and forgot to reply. She could hear children in the background, and a TV.

"Hello?" Inez said again.

"Inez?" Jennifer answered.

It took Inez a moment to speak. "Jen?"

"Yes."

"Where are you?"

"Here."

"Lord…hold on." Inez raised her voice, away from the receiver. "Y'all turn that down. Hurry up!"

Jennifer heard some kids complaining, but then the volume on the TV was lowered.

"Jen. Oh, my Lord."

Jennifer took a deep breath. "How are you?"

"I'm cool, I'm good. How are you?"

"I'm okay," Jennifer answered.

"When did you get here?"

"Last Thursday." Jennifer nervously twirled the yellow cord around her finger. "I was hoping…I would really love to see you."

"Well, come on," Inez answered. "Mama's at work, but she'll be home soon. She's gonna freak out."

"How is she?" Jennifer could see Mama Tyne clearly, in a voluminous checked house dress that didn't conceal her enormous chest or extra hundred pounds, with her hair cut short and curled, always wearing big clip-on earrings.

"She's good," Inez answered. "The same."

"Would today be okay?"

"Girl, get off the phone!"

Milton Street was on the east side of Dismal, only a couple of miles from Grandma's place. At one time, once they were seven or eight and allowed to leave the adults' eyesight, Jennifer and Inez and Jonah had ridden their bikes between the two places. Daniel had come along later, the summer before ninth grade. Jennifer had fallen for him instantly. But she was his buddy's twin sister, so Daniel didn't *really* look at her until they were sophomores.

The neighborhood had changed since Jennifer had seen it last. There were more cars parked in the driveways and on the streets, or at least it seemed that way. Most of the homes were still well-kept, though none of them was remotely fancy. There were a few places whose yards were decorated with cars on blocks, mangy dogs and barbecue grills made out of 55-gallon drums, but there were houses in some of the white neighborhoods that were decorated the same way.

Young men still clustered on the sidewalks, listening to somebody's car radio, smoking cigarettes and drinking cans of Shasta cola and Frostie root beer or Schlitz and Pabst Blue Ribbon. Younger men and older boys moved out of the road as Jennifer drove slowly through their kickball and stickball games. Old men talked over chain-link fences and in pockets of aluminum folding chairs set up in somebody's front yard.

Jennifer was watched as she passed through, sometimes curiously, sometimes cautiously. A few people held a hand up in the traditional Southern greeting.

236 Milton Street was a cinderblock house, still painted light blue, with white rocks in the narrow flowerbeds that lined the front. White aluminum awnings over the jalousie windows, and a sprinkler attached to a garden hose, twirling strings of water that looked like Mardi Gras beads in the sun. Just like eleven or twenty-five years ago, there was a pile of bicycles under the tree out front, though the bikes were different, and the tree was taller.

But when Jennifer parked in the dirt driveway next to a blue, '65 Ambassador, all she saw was Inez.

She had been bent over the sprinkler, one hand on the hose, like she was about to move it. When Jennifer pulled in, Inez straightened up. She dropped the hose, but stood there in the sprinkler, one hand on her cheek.

She was still the most beautiful person Jennifer had ever seen, more beautiful than she'd been at eighteen. She was wearing white cut-offs and a yellow tube top, and her legs were impossibly long. The water glistened on her beautiful brown skin, shone like diamonds in the hair that was still chin-length, but now touched with red and left to its natural, dainty curls.

She still had small breasts and a torso that went on forever. Her hips had widened just a bit, but they just made her waist look even tinier.

She was so beautiful standing there, her almond eyes wide, and without warning, Jennifer burst into tears. Not silent, delicate tears, but great, wracking sobs that made her jaw ache and her chest tighten. She saw Inez shudder, saw her clamp her hand over her mouth, and Jennifer put her own hands over her eyes. A moment later, her car door was jerked open and there was Inez, tears streaming down her face, grabbing at Jennifer's shoulder with both hands.

“Get out the car!” Inez sobbed.

Jennifer half-laughed and half-choked. “I can’t, I think I sprained my boobs!”

Inez, squatting down beside the door, covered her mouth again, laughing and crying. It was an old joke, born when Jennifer was weeping like an idiot on Inez’s shoulder. They were about fifteen, and Jennifer had just heard the mean rumor about Daniel and Liz, which had turned out to be untrue. Inez, always picking on Jennifer for her ample breasts, had made her laugh by telling her if she kept crying like that, she’d sprain her boobs.

Inez swiped at her nose with the back of her hand and pulled a pack of Kools and a matchbook out of her back pocket. “Aw, man. My matches are soaked.”

She pointed in the general direction of Jennifer’s dashboard, and Jennifer punched the lighter in.

“I can’t believe you smoke,” Jennifer said.

Inez grinned. “You would, too, if you were black.” That, too, was an old routine.

They both laughed. The lighter popped out and Jennifer handed it to Inez. She lit her cigarette, then exhaled as she handed it back to Jennifer.

“You want one?” Inez asked once Jennifer had put the lighter back.

“No. I’ve got enough problems.” She watched Inez take a drag. “I can’t believe you’re here.”

“Me?! I live here. I can’t believe *you’re* here.”

Jennifer swiped at her eyes. “I was just calling to talk to Mama Tyne, and get your number.”

Inez nodded, her curls bouncing. “This is gonna blow her mind.”

The last time she and Inez had talked on the phone was in ’65. Inez was in her sophomore year at Howard University, on a full scholarship. Jennifer didn’t have a scholarship, and Aunt Milly hadn’t had any money, so Jennifer was waitressing in the French Quarter to save up for junior college.

“I expected you to be…I don’t know, someplace else,” Jennifer said. “When Grandma came out for Aunt Milly’s funeral, she said you were getting ready to graduate.”

“I was really sorry to hear about Grammy,” Inez said quietly. Jennifer nodded. “Yeah. I did graduate. The kids and I have been back for almost a year.”

It was only then that Jennifer noticed the wedding set on Inez’s long, slender ring finger.

“So, you did get married. The guy from Howard?”

“Morgan. Morgan Johnson. Yeah.”

They looked at each other for a moment, uncomfortably. Jennifer knew they were both thinking about Jonah. Inez had been like a sister to Jennifer. In another world, she would have been her sister-in-law. She forced a smile.

"I'm sure he's great. I can't wait to meet him."

Inez looked down and focused on her cigarette for a moment, flicking at the filter with her coral-painted fingernail. "Girl, get out of the car, I'm gonna get a charley horse."

Inez stood, and Jennifer grabbed her purse and got out. She closed her door as Inez ground out her cigarette.

"I'm looking forward to that, too," Inez said quietly. "He hasn't come back from Vietnam yet." She saw the questions in Jennifer's eyes. "He's listed MIA, but I'm thinking maybe he's one of the POWs they haven't gotten to yet. Every time the news shows another group of men coming home, I watch." She shook her head. "I'm sure there's a lot of men they haven't found or don't have names for yet."

Jennifer smiled, meaning for it to look reassuring. What kind of strength did Inez have, to lose two men? One who had wanted to be her husband and one who was?

"Anyway, we were at Fort Bragg, but it just got to be too much," Inez said. "Chaplain knocking on a different door every day. Every day a different mother of three or nineteen-year-old girl weeping at my kitchen table. I needed to come home. And it helps Mama."

Inez was the oldest of five kids; all but her were boys. She had always been needed at home, even before her father had keeled over from a stroke when the girls were fourteen.

"I can't imagine," Jennifer said, and felt stupid for saying it. They'd been too close for too long to have to spout platitudes.

Inez smiled, then shook her head. "I can't believe you're here."

"Me, neither. It doesn't seem real yet."

"How long are you gonna be here?"

Jennifer swallowed. "I'm staying."

"Are you serious?"

"Yeah."

"Oh, my gosh." Inez shook her head. "Why?"

Jennifer shrugged. "I wanted to come home."

Inez stared at her for a minute. "Does Daniel know?"

"Yeah."

"You seen him?" Inez asked. Jennifer just nodded. "Bad, huh?"

Jennifer shrugged. "Nothing out of line."

"Please," Inez huffed. "Daniel has never been out of line."

"You know what I mean," Jennifer said. "He has every right to hate me."

Inez put her hands on her hips. "He doesn't hate you, Jen. It was just really hard for him for a long time."

Jennifer nodded. Inez had told her that the first few times they'd talked on the phone, after Jennifer had left. But that was too hard, and one time Jennifer had just had to end the call. By unspoken agreement, neither one of them mentioned Daniel again, and eventually, they stopped calling each other, too.

Inez grabbed Jennifer's shoulder. "Oh, girl. Here comes Mama."

They watched as Mama Tyne got out of the back of a black Falcon, and waved as it drove off. Mama Tyne hadn't changed much. She wore a gold and brown caftan, and those plastic sandals older women were wearing, sold in the back of the TV Guide. Easy-somethings that were supposed to be comfortable but looked like Barbie had tightened her budget. On her arm was an enormous brown purse with an assortment of outside pockets.

Mama Tyne frowned at the Dart, then looked up and saw Inez and Jennifer. It took a minute for curiosity to change to recognition. Her mouth dropped open and Jennifer smiled at her nervously. Mama Tyne raised a hand to her mouth.

"Oh, my sweet Jesus Lord," she said without irreverence. "Oh, my—"

She stopped talking and started charging down the driveway, breasts slamming up and down, hands waving in the air beside her ears.

"Yes, Jesus, yes, Lord!" she hollered. "It's my little white baby!"

Mama Tyne arrived, and grabbed up Jennifer so hard and so fast that she didn't get to speak. It wouldn't have mattered, because Jen was crying again, anyway.

"Oh, my Jenny! Oh, my girl!" Mama Tyne was saying over and over, as Jennifer's face was pressed into her bosom.

Jennifer had been lonely for years, but she had forgotten what being in the presence of family felt like, how comforting and grounding it was just to be in the presence of people who loved you. She had mourned for so much, for so many people, but she hadn't realized how alone she had really been. She knew it now, as she wept into Mama Tyne's polyester caftan, breathing in the scent of Jean Naté and baby powder.

"I don't believe it!" Mama Tyne said. "I don't believe you're standing here!"

"Mama, you're killin' her, though," Jennifer heard Inez say.

Jennifer and Mama Tyne sat at a fake-oak kitchen table with tan vinyl chairs on wheels. Mama Tyne had always kept a nice home. Much more furnished and accessorized than Grandma's place. Every surface was covered with figurines, potted plants, or candy dishes, and if Mama Tyne had any more grandchildren, she'd need to get some more walls. All of hers were covered with oil paintings and family photographs.

There were assorted children in the living room, out back, and in the bedrooms, ranging in age from seventeen to two-and-a-half. Jennifer was overwhelmed and couldn't keep them straight when they were introduced, though she knew some were the children of Inez's brothers. There was also an assortment of cousins, nieces and nephews. There always had been. Mama Tyne liked her house to be noisy and full.

The youngest child was Inez's son, Isaac. A serious-looking toddler wearing Garanimals overalls and a tiny afro. Inez's daughter Ruthie was four, with a Josie and the Pussycats T-shirt on and two little braids with purple ribbon. They sat on the carpet in front of a console television in the adjoining living room. Jennifer could hear Big Bird talking sense to somebody.

Inez was standing in front of the fridge with the door open. “We’ve got red Kool-Aid, sweet tea, water or orange juice.”

Jennifer smiled. “I haven’t had Kool-Aid in so long. I’d like that.”

“Mama?”

Mama Tyne was opening one piece of mail while she fanned herself with the other. “Tea, please, baby. Did you take something out for supper?”

“I thawed that chicken,” Inez answered. She put both the tea and a jug of Kool-Aid on the counter, and pulled three avocado-green glasses out of a cupboard.

Mama Tyne looked up from her mail. “You’re eatin’ with us. You look skinny. Who feeds you?”

Jennifer shrugged. “I just feed myself.”

“Well, you’re failing at it. Inez, get her a bowl of those greens to nibble on ’til supper’s ready.”

Mama Tyne had always had at least two pots going on the stove at all times, usually a soup or stew and some greens. No one ever left her house hungry, and they were usually told to eat “a little somethin’” within four minutes of walking in the door.

“It’s okay, I’ll save my appetite for later. I ate lunch.”
Mama Tyne narrowed her eyes at her. “Really.”

Mama Tyne let it go, and Inez brought tea for herself and her mother, and Kool-Aid for Jennifer.

Jennifer hadn't gotten past staring at her yet, and after Inez sat down, she caught Jennifer doing it.

"What?" she said with an uncertain grin.

"You're so beautiful," Jennifer said, shaking her head. "I mean, I remembered that you were, but you're even more beautiful now than you were when we were eighteen."

"So are you!" Inez laughed. "You still don't get that."

"Oh, piffle," Jennifer said.

"And you still talk like Grammy."

Mama Tyne plopped a warm hand over one of Jennifer's. "Have you seen Daniel? Of course you have. Have you seen him?"

"Yeah," she answered vaguely.

"Good, good," Mama Tyne said, patting her hand. "That makes me so happy."

Jennifer and Inez exchanged glances. Jennifer wasn't ready to explain herself and Daniel to Mama Tyne, yet. She just wanted to warm her soul here at this table.

One of Inez's cousins, a girl of about thirteen, came to stand where the green shag carpet of the living room met the tan linoleum of the kitchen.

"What you need, Franny?" Mama Tyne asked.

"Louis is licking the window screen again."

CHAPTER 8

It was after nine and well past dark when Jennifer pulled into her lane. Through the trees, she could see the porch light she'd left on, but she didn't see Daniel's truck until she rounded the curve. She parked beside it, and looked over. He wasn't inside.

She grabbed her purse and a paper bag from the passenger seat. In the bag were pink and yellow Tupperware containers full of leftovers that Mama Tyne had shoved through her car window.

She took a deep breath and got out of the car. When she was halfway up the path to the porch, she saw Daniel sitting on the top step, and she stopped.

He was just sitting there with his elbows on his knees, chewing on a toothpick. He used to take a toothpick from every place they ever went to eat. He had always said it helped him keep his mouth shut.

He was wearing jeans and one of those white Wrangler button-downs with the tails out, and his blue eyes glowed in the dark. She realized in that instant that she had never actually recovered from loving and losing Daniel Evans Huddleston, and she likely never would.

"Hi," she said.

He nodded and twisted the toothpick with his tongue.

"How long have you been here?"

He waved a mosquito away from his ear. "About an hour."

He let the silence expand until she filled it. "Why?" she asked finally.

"What are you doing here, Jen?"

She didn't answer right away. She had expected this question for weeks, but she couldn't remember any of her answers. So, "What do you mean?" she asked.

"What do I mean?" he asked mildly. "I mean you're a cop, and you've come back to the place where your mother and brother and friend were murdered, so what are you doing here?"

"That's not the only reason."

"No?"

"No. It was a lot of things...Grandma and...I wanted to come home."

"Why are you suddenly employed by the Dismal Police Department?"

"Because I'm a cop."

"But why are you a cop *here*, is what I'm asking."

"Because I'm staying." She shrugged her purse strap back up her shoulder. "Yes, I want to know what really happened. I want to look at the cases. But, that's just one of several reasons I came home."

"Have you considered that the people responsible are probably still here?"

"Yes."

He nodded and looked away, chewing at the toothpick.

"I was at Inez's," she said for lack of something else. "She says she hasn't seen you since you caught Leon smoking pot a couple years ago and brought him home."

"Little Leon's old enough to smoke grass, can you believe that?" he asked quietly. It wasn't really a question, and she didn't answer. "I've arrested Willie a few times," he said, meaning her father. "Drunk and disorderly, peeing on the front door of Woolworth's in the middle of the night, that kind of thing."

Jennifer felt a tendril of shame wrap around her throat. That had been one of the reasons she hadn't stayed, or let him come with her, even if he could have. His family was so clean and whole, and her family was not. Her mother was an activist, her father was a drunk, and they had to live with her grandmother to get by.

Not once had Daniel or anyone in his family ever made her feel like they were better than she was, but that had just proven to her young mind that they were. Especially once people started murdering her family.

"How is Inez?" he asked.

She walked slowly over to the porch steps. When she got there, she could smell Jovan Musk. She used to buy it for him every birthday.

She sat down on the middle step, the paper bag in her lap. "She's good. She has two beautiful children." He blinked at her a few times. "Her husband hasn't come back from Vietnam."

"I know." His toothpick stopped moving, and he stared at her a moment. "I kept your senior picture taped to the inside of my helmet for two years, did you know that?"

It was her turn to stare.

"I didn't know you were in Vietnam," she managed to say. Retroactive fear for his wellbeing swallowed her whole.

"'66 to '68," he said, sounding so casual about it. "Your Grandma said there was no reason for you to be scared until there was something to be scared about." He looked away for a moment before he spoke again. "I had my dad mail it to me, after I was in-country for about six months. And I taped it in my cover because when you're over there it's like no other reality exists."

He took the toothpick out and looked at it, rolled it over a few times, then put the other end in his mouth. "I was starting to forget that the real world was here, not there. Even if you weren't in it."

"I wish you hadn't been there," Jennifer said quietly.

"I wish none of us had been there." He tossed the toothpick into the grass. "Not even them."

He stood up and stretched. "So, I smell that Mama Tyne is still a heck of a cook."

Jennifer stood. "Yeah. Are you hungry?"

"No," he answered, shaking his head.

"There's plenty," she said weakly. "Between Inez's kids and the siblings and cousins and whatnot, there were eleven people in that house, and they still had leftovers."

He was staring at her again, and he was so close that she was having trouble breathing. She hadn't been that close to him in over a decade, and she had forgotten *exactly* how he smelled and sounded and all of his expressions. She had forgotten that he had a tiny white scar by his left ear. He got it falling off her handlebars, when they were messing around. And now he was so close and it was like seeing him again and also seeing him for the first time.

"I have to go," he said shortly, and started down the steps.

"Wait," she said, and he stopped on the bottom step, which put them eye to eye.

"I didn't think you should leave, but you definitely shouldn't have come back," he said.

"I know. But, I needed to leave. And I needed to come back."

He nodded. "Yeah, well, that's the hell of the thing, right?" He turned and started walking away. "I'll tell David and Audrey and little Danny that you said 'hello,'" he said without turning around. "Remember them?"

It punched her right in the chest. She remembered vividly. It was just a few months before she'd left. They were just fooling around with his mother's baby names book.

He was already at his truck before she found her breath, dropped her purse and the bag of leftovers and ran down the steps. He had just closed his door when she got there. He looked at her when she slapped the side of his truck.

"That was so *unkind*!" she yelled.

"I didn't say it to hurt you. Yes, I did. I wanted to hurt you. But what you probably won't believe is that that's not all there is to it."

His face was so close to hers that she could feel his breath, warm and humid, on her cheeks.

"Daniel, please don't leave yet—"

He started his engine, then sat back. He looked at her as he shifted into reverse, and he didn't look angry. He just looked sad. "Jennifer, everything that we could have said or done, well, we already missed that."

She watched him drive away, her arms hugging her waist. Then she walked back to the porch, picked up her things, and opened the door. Below and beyond the scraping of the wooden door against the floorboards, she heard another sound.

She stopped, her hand on the door knob. She stood there and stared at the floor without seeing it, and listened. From somewhere behind her, in the woods between the side of the house and the road, she heard a branch snap.

She calmly walked inside, shut the door, and turned the useless door knob lock that was only there because people were supposed to have some sort of lock on their doors. The lock was so flimsy that it hardly mattered.

She slid her purse from her shoulder and set the bag down on the floor, then made her way across the living room in the dark. Only a few days, and she already remembered how to move through the house in total darkness.

She went through the living room, turned right into the short hall of the addition. As she passed the bathroom, she heard rustling through the open window. She didn't pause, just kept walking normally, into her room.

She walked to the nightstand, and slowly pulled out the little drawer, the one that tended to stick. The only thing in it was her revolver. There was a window just above the nightstand, and another one on the south wall. The curtains on that window lifted just barely in the slight breeze. She looked back down at the drawer and closed her eyes, shutting out the visual to enhance the audible.

She waited for over a minute, hand hovering over her weapon, eyes closed, the breeze from the window brushing a wisp of hair against her forehead.

She waited and she thought that she hadn't locked the kitchen door, because she had never locked it in her life, but it didn't matter. The door was dozens of feet away and creaked terribly. Her hand was less than six inches from the Chiefs Special.

Female police officers worked twice as hard as men to excel, needing to excel at something, at anything, to be accepted. To survive. And she had excelled at marksmanship.

She waited for three minutes or more, without moving. Listening. To nothing else. Then she took her gun with her as she walked to the kitchen in the dark, turned the lock in the kitchen door knob, and then went to bed in her shorts and T-shirt, her gun beside her pillow.

Suddenly, Jennifer was already back by the lake, staring at Ned's father's 1959 Galaxie. Jennifer heard the roar of an engine, and tires on gravel, but this time she didn't look up to see the taillights disappearing around the bend.

First, she saw the back of Ned's head, leaning against the window frame. Blood that made no sense in Jennifer's world was running down the side of the driver's door. Then she realized that Inez was yelling over the car radio, which Ned had been blasting. That week's hottest song, "The Locomotion", which seemed so inappropriate, already.

"Jonah!" Inez was screaming from somewhere.

Jennifer ran to the driver's side and yanked open the back door.

He was lying on his side and his eyes were wide open. The most beautiful blue eyes she'd ever seen. There was blood on the back of his neck, and on the seat beneath him.

In her sleep, Jennifer held her breath. No, it's not supposed to be Daniel!

"No," Jennifer said. "No," she kept saying. She was almost grunting the word. The sound reminded some part of her brain of a mama bear, warning away some danger.

She dropped to her knees, barely feeling the gravel cutting into her skin.

Daniel's eyes were wide open, and she hoped they were the last thing she would ever see.

CHAPTER 9

Jennifer's first morning with the Dismal, Florida Police Department started pretty much as she'd expected, though she hadn't bothered to try to predict the exact details. Her shift started at six. She was up at three because she was too nervous to sleep any longer. She walked into the station with a red plaid Thermos of coffee just after five-thirty.

She was disappointed to learn that Ray wasn't in. Sgt. Stewart Michaels, the gray-haired officer who had expressed his polite concern about lady cops, was the supervising officer for night shift. He advised her that the Chief was on his way to Chipley for a meeting with the sheriff of neighboring Washington County. Michaels had been polite enough, if not friendly, and Jennifer was grateful for that.

There was only one locker room, so Jennifer came to work fully dressed. Most of the guys who started trickling in did, too, though a few came in street clothes, grabbed some coffee, and went to the lockers to change.

Jennifer had gone straight from Sgt. Michaels' desk to her own. She and Messer had the two desks in the east corner. Messer had a big jar of Kraft caramels on his desk, along with a picture of himself and a very pretty young woman with white-blond hair and a warm smile.

By 5:40, Daniel still wasn't there, and neither was Messer. Jennifer didn't really feel like having to speak to or walk through the other day shift guys, but she'd had a glass of water and two cups of coffee before leaving the house, and she needed to use the restroom.

She got up, feeling most or all eyes on her, and was relieved to see a woman enter the bullpen. She was a slightly chubby, older lady with a cap of tight, gray curls, and though she wore a brown polyester shift dress, she had a department name tag on her chest and a paper cup in her hand.

They met a few feet from the coffee table.

"Oh, hi," the woman said. "You must be 232."

"I'm sorry, what?"

"Your call number. Yours and Messer's unit is 19, but he's 219 and you're 232. I'm Maureen, one of the dispatchers."

"It's nice to meet you," Jennifer said, and the older woman nodded as she started to fill her coffee cup. "Hey, can you tell me where the ladies' room is?"

"Yeah, sure, it's—"

"She wants to be a cop, she needs to use the cops' facilities," said a male voice behind them.

They both turned to see the redheaded cop, Whitney, standing there with a small paper sack that smelled of cinnamon rolls.

"Shut up, Norman, I play bridge with your mother," Maureen said. She looked back at Jennifer. "It's out front, off the lobby, down that hall to the left."

"Thank you," Jennifer replied, then sidestepped Whitney to head for the door.

Patterson, the blond cop who was worried about Jennifer's menstrual cycle, winked at her as he was coming in and she was going out. She ignored him.

When she walked back to her desk, she found a gift waiting for her on her nearly empty desk. She heard a few chuckles behind her as she looked at the disconcertingly-large pink vibrator that was standing at attention next to her Thermos. She took a tissue from the box on Messer's desk, picked up the vibrator and turned back the way she'd come.

She was distracted from Patterson's smirk by Daniel's entrance. As they approached each other, his eyes shot from her to the object in her hands, and his expression went from alarm to curiosity and anger. He didn't say anything, though, as he passed her. Neither did she.

She stopped at Patterson's desk and smiled as she stood the vibrator up on his desk. "Your wife will be wanting this back," she said politely, then turned around with an accompaniment of laughter, some cautious, some heartier. She heard Daniel's gentle laughter in the mix.

She bumped into Messer, who had apparently just walked in. He had a wide smile on his face. "Sheehan, I said to pack a *lunch*!"

There was more laughter this time, and this time Jennifer joined in, her deep, husky laugh a genuine one. She'd always wished it had been daintier, more feminine.

"If you're done playing with your little friends, it's almost muster," Messer said as they walked to their desks.

She glanced over at Daniel. He was smiling at his pencil cup.

"Anyway, Michelle's dad loaned us the down payment on the trailer, and we really want to pay him back, but do you know how expensive it is to give birth?"

"No, now that you mention it." Jen took a sip from her Thermos. "So, is that where your wife is from, too? Defuniak Springs?"

"No, she's from here," he answered. "I'm originally from Pensacola. We moved to the Springs when I was fourteen, when Pop got out of the Navy."

"So, it's still going to be expensive? Even with PD insurance?"

"Like buying another car," Messer said. "So, she's been working nights over at Zayre's until a couple weeks ago. They were really pressuring her to go home. Said it didn't look good for her to be at a cash register at seven months."

"They're probably worried her water will break during the Fourth of July sale," Jennifer said, smiling.

"That's what she said!" Messer slapped at his steering wheel.

There had been no discussion about who would drive, though Jennifer headed for the passenger side before he went to the driver's. Her last partner hadn't let her drive at all. She figured Messer might, but he didn't need too much change on his first day with her.

"You know, I just realized why I was kind of glad the chief assigned me to be your partner. I mean, besides the fact that you probably won't fart me into a coma like Murray did, pardon the biology."

He had already explained that his former partner, Kenneth Murray, had retired two months earlier.

"Okay, so why?"

"Well, it's because you're a woman, but not because you're pretty, although you're a knock-out, if you don't mind me saying that."

"Okay," she said.

"What I mean is, you're a very attractive person, but you're not my type, even though you and Michelle are both blonds. Oh, crap, that sounded terrible!" he said, as Jennifer laughed.

"Thanks so much, partner."

"No, no. Look, I'm sorry. What I mean is, there's nobody in the world that can touch Michelle. I can see that another woman is really pretty the way I see that a new boat or the beach is pretty. But I haven't seen a *beautiful* woman since my third date with my wife."

"That's really nice," Jennifer said with a pang of envy. She was not that woman to anyone.

"She'll like you," he said. He looked over at her. "I'd appreciate it if you'd come over to eat when she invites you. It'll make her feel better."

"What do you mean?"

"Okay, look. She's already asked me how old you are, what you look like, that kind of thing," he shrugged. "You know, like a woman asks about another woman who's spending time with her husband. We do the same thing, us guys. We're just clumsier about it."

"Anthony—is it okay if I just call you Anthony?" He shrugged. "If me being your partner is going to make her feel funny, I'm happy to talk to her."

"Yeah, yeah," he said. "I was honest with her. I said you were a little younger than us, and that you were blond, and yes you were pretty. I don't lie to my wife, unless she asks me if I know where her Count Chocula went, okay?"

Jennifer laughed. "She knows you ate it, Anthony."

"She *thinks* maybe I did, but her hormones are all messed up, so she thinks *maybe* she finished it off." He raised his eyebrows at her. "I've been married four years, okay? Anyway, she's not a jealous woman. Her self-confidence is just a little shaky because of the pregnancy. Once she meets you, she'll like you, and she'll feel fine."

"I'd really like to meet her," Jennifer said. "I have a really close girlfriend here, but it's been a long time since I've been home. I don't really know many people anymore."

“Cool.” He drove in silence for a moment, then he glanced over at her a couple times.

“What?” she asked him.

“I can shut up. But…so, you and Daniel, then?”

There was that dull ache in her chest, which wasn’t as dull as it had been a month ago, or even last week. “That was a long time ago. High school.”

“So?”

“So, what?”

“I really like Daniel, he’s a stand-up guy,” Messer said.

“He is,” Jennifer said to the window.

“Now that he’s single again, maybe you guys can rekindle or something.”

They were at the stoplight, and Jennifer was so grateful to already be staring at a fire hydrant. She even felt pale, so if Messer could have seen her face, she would have had humiliation to add to shock.

“He’s divorced?” she asked as casually as she could manage.

“Oh, Anthony your mouth,” he said quietly. “Hey, Sheehan. Jennifer, look, I’m really sorry.”

She looked over at him quickly, and gave him a smile that she hoped looked better than it felt. “Why? It’s okay. Really.”

But it wasn’t. It was ridiculous for her to feel anything other than a bit of regret for what might have been, like a normal adult would. They had been eighteen. Seniors in high school. Yes, they had made plans to marry. She had had a ring.

"I can't just not explain, but please don't tell Daniel where you heard it."

Messer looked so upset when she turned to look at him that she started feeling sorry for him instead of herself. "I won't," she said.

"He was engaged to Susan somebody; I forget her last name," Messer said. "She's Pastor Huddleston's assistant. You know, his dad. They broke it off a year or so ago."

Jennifer nodded for no particular reason. "Okay," she said simply, hoping she sounded like she was talking about the weather. In actuality, she just couldn't help feeling like her cat died.

But it was eleven years ago. He wasn't a senior in high school; he was a grown man, and grown men had lives that included grown women.

Late that first afternoon, Jennifer and Messer responded to a fender bender call on her old street. She'd been relieved that it was a few blocks shy of their old house, but her relief was short-lived. They had just sent the tow truck off and cleared the last of the looky-loos when she turned around and looked into the eyes of her father.

William "Willie" Sheehan had aged twenty-five years in the last eleven. His slack, splotchy skin and broken capillaries were a testament to his heavy drinking, and he'd shed at least twenty pounds from an already-slim frame. His green eyes were rheumy, and his graying brown hair badly needed cutting. He was wearing baggy trousers and a formerly-white T-shirt underneath an open short-sleeved shirt. He looked like dozens of men that she had arrested.

"Jennifer," he said quietly. There was surprise in his eyes, though perhaps less than there would have been if he had been sober.

"Dad," she said politely. She glanced behind her and saw Messer watching them from where he stood leaning on his open door.

"You look really good, hon. You look fine," he said. "But you shouldn't be here."

"Well, I am," she answered, and looked pointedly at her watch.

"You should go back wherever you were," he said. "You're too good for this place, and it's not safe for you here."

"I'm fine."

"Aw, no, you know it's not safe for you here. I couldn't stand it if something happened to you, too."

Jennifer blew out a breath. By the looks of him, he wouldn't be able to stand it if *anything* happened to *anybody*.

"I have to get back to work," she said. "Take care of yourself."

He had his mouth open to answer, but didn't have a chance to do it. She turned on her heel and got into the car. Messer got in after her.

When they pulled away, Jennifer glanced in her side mirror and saw her father, looking pitiful, watching them go. Messer didn't say anything right away, so she addressed the issue first, to keep it from becoming more uncomfortable for Messer than it already was.

"My father," she said unnecessarily.

"Yeah, I know him, but I didn't make the connection."

Jennifer looked over at him and tried to smile. "Don't feel too bad. I'm used to people knowing my father is an alcoholic. He has been since I was pretty small."

"That had to be tough," he said sympathetically.

She shrugged. "Sometimes. He and my mother split when Jonah and I were nine. My mom said he was never really the same after he came back from Korea, but I do have some good memories of him. Mainly from before the war."

She got a picture in her head of standing on her father's feet as they waltzed in the living room of their old house. She did have some good memories, and that one was one of the few.

"Your mom ever remarry?" Messer asked.

"No, she was too busy with marches and petitions and sit-ins and whatnot," she answered. "I don't think she trusted her own judgement, anyway. She had really fallen for my dad, when she was nineteen. But she realized pretty quickly that he was handsome, but he was also insecure and stupid with money and drank a little more than she'd realized. When he came back from Korea, I guess it was worse. So, we moved in with my grandmother and Mom got a divorce."

Messer nodded. "That's too bad. Maybe one of these days he'll straighten up."

Jennifer smiled. "Maybe."

But she doubted that very much. Her father had still been living in their old house when Jonah died, but she had no idea how he'd hung onto it, since he couldn't keep a job. At Jonah's funeral, his state had actually frightened her. He had been completely broken, and Uncle Ray had taken him home before the service was over. Willie didn't make it to his ex-wife's funeral. He'd been in the hospital, recovering from a three-day bender.

If there had been any promise left in her father, she never saw it after he lost his son and his wife within two weeks of each other.

Daniel hadn't come back to the station yet when Messer and Jennifer finished up their paperwork for the day. Apparently, he was hung up with a bar fight across town at a dive called Lester's.

Jennifer politely declined Messer's offer to stop by and meet his wife, and Ray's offer to go home with him for dinner.

As she unlocked her car door and stood there waiting for the interior to cool off, she stared at Daniel's truck parked several spaces away. When she finally got in her car and drove away, she felt a hollowness in her gut. It wasn't just loneliness, but a feeling of utter aloneness, one that wouldn't have been eliminated by hiding herself away for an hour in the more populated lives of others.

CHAPTER 10

When they got into their cruiser the next morning, Messer spent the first fifteen minutes griping about the ribbing he was taking from the other guys about having Jennifer for a partner. Jennifer felt a little badly about it, but he seemed to take it in stride. A little complaining got it out of his system, and he assured her that he enjoyed her company and saw quite a few benefits in having her as a partner.

"The thing is, I can talk to you about female stuff, stuff that's going on with Michelle, you know, like that, and you'll actually get it."

Jennifer laughed. "Are you sure? Some men, especially cops, think that if a woman's a cop, she's probably not a real woman."

"That's a load of crap."

They turned onto Claiborne Street and drove slowly past the elementary school. School was out, but there were quite a few kids on the playground, and a few riding their bikes in the parking lot.

"So, why are you so liberal?" Jennifer asked him

"Me? I don't think I'm all that liberal. Maybe compared to Patterson or Whitney or a lot of other guys, but what kind of comparison is that?" He pulled a stick of Fruit Stripes gum from the well under the dash. "You want some?"

"Sure." Jennifer took the gum and he grabbed another for himself. She held a hand out for his wrapper, and put both wrappers in the ash tray.

"But you're fine with women being police officers, or at least with me," Jennifer said. "That's kind of progressive, whether you think of yourself that way or not."

"Look, I don't read *Ms.* magazine or anything," Messer said. "But it just never seemed normal to me to treat ladies like that. I mean, I wouldn't talk to my mom or my sister like she was a prostitute or an idiot, so why some other woman?"

Jennifer smiled at him. "Well, then, as partners go, I guess you'll do."

"Well, before you go telling people I'm the Dick Cavett of Dismal PD, you should know that fags scare the crap out of me and I don't have one black friend."

"Why is that?"

"The fags?"

"No black friends," Jennifer said.

"Because not everybody was raised by a civil rights activist that let her white son date a black girl, you know what I mean?"

Jennifer's smile dimmed a bit. "You did some poking around. Or was everybody just dying to tell you over at Monty's?"

"I don't have the extra dollar to go to Monty's," Messer said as he put on his turn signal. "But some of the guys remembered you, remembered what happened. They were talking about it."

"What did they say?"

He looked at her, his brows pulling together a bit.

"It won't bother me," she said.

"Okay. Well, they said that back in '62, you and a black girlfriend were out at the lake with Coach Gilliam's kid, Ted—"

"Ned."

"Sorry, Ned. And your brother, who some of the guys said was seeing the black girl."

"He was," she replied.

"That took guts in '62."

"Well, yeah. But at the time, only our families knew about it. And a couple of close friends, like poor Ned. He was such a sweet, funny guy." Jennifer took the gum out of her mouth, tucked it into the wrapper, and put the wrapper back in the ash tray. "Our family and Inez's—that's my friend—were close for years. Her father used to work for my grandfather, and even though they had the race thing and twenty years between them, they were best friends."

"That's cool. Me, I'll admit I'm not attracted to black women. I'm not attracted to short women or curly-haired women, either. I'm just saying I don't think it's that big a deal. Different strokes for different folks."

Jennifer swallowed and nodded, looking out the window, watching for anything out of the way or anyone needing help.

"Anyway. I heard that both of the guys got shot. Killed. And that a couple weeks later you found your mom…deceased. Murdered."

Jennifer nodded. "Yes."

"I don't even wanna know how hard that was."

She shrugged. "I got through it."

There was no point in boring him, or embarrassing herself, by telling him just how hard that had been, and how lost she'd gotten along the way.

The rest of Jennifer's first week was fairly uneventful. There were fewer and fewer nasty comments by the other officers, and there were no more sex toys or other gifts meant to embarrass her. Whether this was due to the stern talk Ray had had with the guys at the end of her first day, or out of respect for Daniel, she didn't know.

Jennifer and Messer did encounter quite a few sidelong glances and silly comments about "lady cops," "girl cops," and so on, but they both took it in stride. Jennifer had been used to it for quite a while, and Messer just didn't care a whole lot about what other people thought.

Outside of morning muster and the shift change, Jennifer didn't see Daniel again until Thursday.

She walked into Ray's office at the end of the day. He was on the telephone, apparently arranging to have his car serviced, and held up a finger. She sat down to wait.

"Hey, Jennifer," he said after he'd hung up. "How'd your shift go?"

"Good. It went fine," she said. "Quiet."

"I think you'll find policing in Dismal to be a far cry from policing in New Orleans," he said smiling. "For one thing, there's no such thing as undercover here. No matter where you go, *somebody* knows you."

"Yeah, I haven't exactly been invisible this week, either. If it's not the fact that I'm a woman, it's the fact that I'm Jennifer Marie Sheehan, come home to rub salt in old wounds."

"Ah, there's some that feel that way, I'm sure. What happened back then, not just to Claire and the boys, but to all kinds of people, black and white, well, lots of people are ashamed. They'd just as soon keep those memories put up. Not that we're all the way past that, but Dismal is certainly way ahead of where it was then."

"I know," Jennifer said. "And I'm fine. There've been plenty of people who welcomed me home, or at least left me alone."

"Good, good."

Jennifer watched him straighten the papers on his desk. "So, you told me to give myself time to settle in—"

"Jennifer. It's been less than two weeks."

"I'm settled," she replied politely. "It's just a file."

"You and I both know it's not just a file."

The murders of Ned Gilliam, Jonah Sheehan and Claire Quindlen had been treated as one case, the obvious connection being Claire's unpopular activities in support of civil rights.

"Uncle Ray, don't you want to know? If you can?"

"Of course, I do, hon." Ray stopped clearing his desk. "I did then. I was just a police officer then, and I wasn't allowed to have anything to do with the case, of course, but I made sure the officers working that case kept me updated."

He took his reading glasses off and slid them into his shirt pocket, then rubbed at his eyes. When he spoke again, his voice was quiet and wistful. "She was like a sister to me, Claire was. You know that."

"I know, Uncle Ray." She sat forward in her chair. When she did, she saw Daniel pass the open door. He glanced in at her, but kept moving. "Ray, this is really important to me. It's important *for* me."

"You realize it's no longer a case, right? Not unless something new comes to light, or someone comes forward after all these years."

"Yes, I know that."

He sighed, then looked at her for a long time. "Give me until tomorrow, so I can remove the photographs from the two scenes."

"Why?"

"Why? You don't need to see those things, Jennifer."

"But, I already did, remember?"

He caught her coming out of the file room. She'd taken three steps down the hall when Daniel grabbed her elbow and steered her in to the supply room.

"What are you doing?" he hissed at her.

"Nothing."

He looked pointedly at the thick brown case file in her hands.

"I heard you talking to the chief. What's wrong with you?" he snapped.

"I didn't do anything wrong," Jennifer snapped back, her voice hushed. "I have Ray's permission!"

"I know that," he replied. "But why don't you just put an affidavit on the bulletin board, saying that the officers on that case weren't smart enough or thorough enough to do a good job? Or worse, that they did a crappy job on purpose because these people got what they deserved?"

"Ray was here then, and I'm not doing this because I think I'm smarter or because I think they swept it under the rug."

"Maybe you are and maybe they did," Daniel said, his hands on his gun belt. "My point is that you don't need anyone else knowing you're looking at this file, because then everybody knows, including the officers who had the case, the cleaning lady, and probably the third cousin of one of the guys that did this."

Jennifer looked at him a minute. He was right, of course. "I know that," she said. "I'm not broadcasting it."

"You're not?" he asked, eyebrows raised.

He looked around, then dumped a few packages of toilet paper out of a brown paper bag from Kash n' Karry. He took the file from her, put it in the bag, and then rolled the top of the bag down.

"Now you're not, maybe." He gave it back to her.

He stalked out of the room and turned left, toward the locker room. Jennifer went right, took the bag back to her desk, and got ready to leave for the day.

CHAPTER 11

Two hours later, as dusk was heading in, Jennifer took a break from trying to drill the last two screws on her new slide bolt for the front door. She stood in the doorway, plucking her T-shirt away from her chest as she tried to catch a breeze through the screen door. The sky was gray and looked like it was only five feet off the ground. She welcomed the promise of a storm.

She was standing there, T-shirt in one hand and drill in the other, when Daniel's truck appeared on her drive. She sighed as she watched him park. He stalked up the path in jeans and a denim shirt, and his hiking boots thumped loudly as he came up the porch steps.

He stopped at the screen door.

"Another thing," he said. "Don't even think about going around asking questions about this. If you have a question, ask Ray; he probably knows the answer. But you can't discuss that case with anybody, you know that, right?"

"As a matter of fact, I do know that," she snapped. "And don't forget that I've been a cop for almost six years."

"You were a meter maid and a dispatcher for four of those years," he snapped back. "But it's not about whether you're a cop or a civilian; it's about wandering around a small town where, even if the guys who did this are dead or gone, they probably have friends and relatives here, and those people aren't going be real excited about you poking around."

She let out a breath. "I know that, Daniel," she said more calmly.

"Well," he said. "Then, that's it." Instead of leaving, though, he popped his fists on his hips and glanced at the drill. "What are you doing?"

"I'm putting a bolt on."

"Why?"

"Because I don't have the round saw thing to make a hole for a deadbolt."

"No, why are you putting new locks on the door?"

"I've just gotten used to having them." She shrugged. "New Orleans is a door-locking kind of town."

He squinted at her a bit, then pulled open the screen door and looked at the back of the heavy wooden front door. She had been in the process of trying to unscrew and re-screw the third screw she'd screwed up.

"You leave those screws like that, and there won't be any point in sliding that bolt," he said.

"I know how to use a drill," she said.

"No, you don't. I'm the one who tried to teach you."

He took the drill from her and she had to step back as he came all the way in.

He reversed the drill and took out the third screw, then gently restarted it, and drilled it in nice and neat. He glanced over at her, then picked up another screw from the packaging on the end table.

He was too close, though he didn't really have any room to give her. She watched his profile as he drilled in the fourth screw. She had always loved his jawline, and the way his blond hair got darker at the ends on a hot day, and curled slightly underneath his ears. She stood there watching him from eight inches away, and wished it would have been okay to lean in and put her face in his neck like she used to love to do.

He was the same Daniel, and not. He was older, with more than ten years of life and memories between the boy she remembered and the man standing next to her. He was also more interesting, and more attractive, than he'd been when they were together. That made her sad. She wished she had watched him become that man.

He finished with the screw and glanced over at her. She would have loved to have been looking somewhere else, but it was too late. He stood there for a moment, hunched over and eye to eye with her, and the blueness of his eyes, the frank honesty there, made her chest hurt. After a moment, he handed her the drill.

"Thank you," she said, and hoped she didn't look as embarrassed as she felt.

"You're welcome."

They looked at each other until she was about to fidget, so she leaned over and unplugged the drill, then started wrapping up the cord.

"I don't hate you, Jen," he said finally.

She wasn't sure what to say to that. That he had a right to? That she was glad he didn't? That she believed that?

"You can't go around giving people the impression that this case has been re-opened," he said quietly.

"I'm not. I'm really not. It's more for me than anything else. I just want to know more tomorrow than I do today."

She grabbed her trash from the floor and, carrying it and the drill, headed for the kitchen. She heard Daniel behind her. Once in the kitchen, she tossed the trash into the can under the sink, then put the drill in the laundry room, on a shelf over the fairly new, Harvest Gold washer.

When she walked back out, Daniel was in the middle of the kitchen, staring at the brown accordion file on the kitchen table.

"Have you looked at it?" he asked her.

"Not yet. As much as I've wanted to see it, I also don't."

She'd left the box and wrapping from the back-door lock on the counter, and she busied herself by throwing them away, too.

"What's the deal with the locks?" he asked her.

"I've been in New Orleans for over ten years. I'm not used to being out in the woods anymore. At least not alone." It was mostly true, if not truthful. She didn't know why she didn't want to be straight with Daniel. Maybe because she'd hate to mistake concern for something else.

"Where do you keep your weapon?"

"In the drawer by my bed."

He nodded, then looked back at the file. "You need a dog."

"I need some tea," she said, turning to the fridge. "Do you want some?"

He hesitated. "Okay."

He stood there, awkwardly, in the middle of the room, while she got the Tupperware jug of tea out and poured them each a glass. She handed him his, then she sat down at the table. He hesitated a bit, then sat down in the chair on her right, the one facing the window. The one he'd always sat in. After school, before the drive-in, on rainy Saturday afternoons. Grandma had adored Daniel.

They both took sips of their tea. They both looked at the file and then tried not to look at it again. She stared at the middle of the table and saw more tuna fish lunches, late-night Cokes and rainy-day card games than she could count. She wondered if he saw the same thing. They'd laughed a lot together in this room. Everyone had.

He looked at her. "Are you going to look at it tonight?"

"I guess I might as well. It's not going to be easier tomorrow."

"I'd like to see it," he said quietly. "If you don't mind me staying."

She looked at those blue eyes and saw compassion, but she also saw curiosity and stubbornness.

“Okay,” she said. She pulled the file closer, and undid the elastic band.

The file expanded a bit as it was loosed, but it wasn’t particularly thick, especially for three murders. There were three sections of paperwork, one for each victim. Each consisted of a stack of paperclipped documents, with stiffer pages at the back that were obviously eight by ten photographs.

At the time, it had seemed very clear to the officers who worked the case, and pretty much everyone else, that the murders were related. Once Claire Quindlen was killed, the theory had been that both Claire and Jonah had been killed for Claire’s civil rights activities. A week and a half later, Jennifer was standing at the airport in New Orleans with a light blue Samsonite and an overwhelming sense of loss.

She decided not to choose, and just pulled out the first stack of paperwork. It was her mother’s file. A basic information form was on top. Claire Elizabeth Quindlen. Born June 4, 1924. The dates struck Jennifer oddly. She’d always thought of her mother as a middle-aged woman. A beautiful middle-aged woman, but middle-aged nonetheless. Yet, she wasn’t. She’d just turned thirty-eight when she was killed. Barely seven years older than Jennifer was now.

The next page was the official autopsy report, with the outline of a woman with arms outstretched, front and back, that looked nothing like her mother. There were notes and lines drawn near and on the figure.

She pulled the paper clip from the stack, slid out the first picture, and felt the hairs on her arms and neck stand up. It was a fairly close shot of her mother sitting behind the steering wheel of their old Rambler. Just like Jennifer remembered, only in black and white.

Out of the corner of her eye, she saw Daniel slide the scene report toward him.

She swallowed and made herself look at the photograph the way she'd looked at others, though not many others. The staring eyes with no warmth in them. The red petechiae in and around the eyes that looked like dark freckles in black and white. The bruising around the throat. The bloody scratches on both sides of her neck, which Jennifer now knew had been put there by Claire herself, fighting to loosen her killer's fingers.

The picture was too close to show it, but Jennifer also knew that Claire had one foot outside the open door, and that both of her heels had come off in the struggle. She knew, too, that her mother had been wearing the charm bracelet that Jonah and Jennifer had given her the Mother's Day before.

Jennifer let out a slow breath, then started laying the photos out in rows of five. There were far fewer pictures than Jennifer had expected, based on her very limited experience with murder cases. Maybe it was because she was the daughter of the once vital and beautiful woman splayed in the front seat of the old car, but she couldn't help thinking that such a cataclysmic, life-changing event should have been documented with rolls upon rolls of film, and better pictures, to boot.

She stared at each picture in turn, and though he was silent, she knew Daniel was doing the same.

"I think I forgot how pretty she really was," he said finally.

"Me, too." She sighed. "You'd think my memories of her would be really clear, but they're not. I mean, some are, but she was always going. She was always attending some rally or sit-in or meeting or something." She looked up quickly, afraid she sounded self-centered. "I know what she was trying to do was important. I was proud of her. I am proud of her. But she wasn't around very much those last few years."

She looked back down at the photographs of the mother who wasn't going to be around again at all. As her eyes drifted around a couple of the pictures of the inside of the car, something tried to catch her attention. She went back to the first picture, trying to figure out what it was.

Nothing jumped out at her about the marks on her mother's neck, or anything else about her body, other than the obvious and distressing fact that the body was her mother, her Mom, the woman who had braided her hair, taught her to tie her shoes, and sternly advised her to be careful about compromising herself when she was alone with Daniel.

Her mother's progressiveness about race had not carried over into her feelings about teens having sex and, of course, Daniel's father was a pastor. Even so, there had been many times especially that last year, when she and Daniel had come pretty darn close to compromising the standards with which they'd been raised. Sometimes it had made her ashamed, sometimes it had excited her. She'd been young and in love, full of hormones and a teenaged girl's certainty that she knew her own future.

"Can I see the autopsy report?" Daniel asked.

Jennifer looked up from the photos, her face warming with the idea that he could read her mind. They used to joke that he could. It wouldn't be as funny now.

She slid the autopsy report over to him, grateful that it took any attention away from her. Then she turned back to the photos. What was it that had seemed to wave at her, asking to be noticed? She went over each picture as slowly as she could make herself do, but if there had been something, it seemed to be too tiny to catch on purpose.

"What did you do when you found your mom?" he asked her, and she looked up. He was focused on the pictures again, the two pages of autopsy results forgotten in his hands. “I mean, was her door open like that or did you open it? Was her leg outside of the car when you got there?”

Jennifer felt like a spider who’d been out in the cold was creeping up her backbone.

“I touched her,” she said. “I didn’t realize she was—her arm wasn’t hanging down like that until I grabbed her. It was hung up on the steering wheel. I mean, her arm was through the steering wheel.”

She looked out the window, not wanting to see her mother, not wanting to see pity on Daniel’s face as she remembered.

“When Mama Tyne went to drop me off in front of Mom’s shop, the lights were on, and we could see the back half of Mom’s car parked in back. Mama Tyne said she’d wait for me to get inside, but the front door was locked—I knew it would be, because Mom always kept it locked at night, well, daytime, too, after the lake. But Mom didn’t come to the door, so I walked around back.”

Jen watched a squirrel dash up the trunk of the apple tree outside the kitchen window. He shook his tail like he was waving at her, or waving her away.

“When I saw Mom’s door open, and her leg sticking out, I thought she was just getting in or getting out. But she didn’t answer me when I said something to her, and then I was by her door, and I saw.”

She looked away from the squirrel, looked down at the table without seeing the photographs. "I saw her face, but I didn't get it right away. I grabbed her arm, and she was so cold. Too cold for the night. Her arm fell, or I dropped it, whatever, and I started screaming. Then Mama Tyne was there, and I don't remember a whole lot about what happened right after."

She looked up at Daniel, who was staring at the pictures on the table. "Except that someone called you, because you showed up at Grandma's a few minutes after Mama Tyne and Inez brought me home."

They had sat right there, at that same table. Grandma constantly wiping her eyes and popping up to get her more hot tea or a cold washcloth. Looking back, Jennifer guessed that taking care of her had been Grandma's way of holding it together. Once the police, Mama Tyne and Inez, and Daniel's father were gone, Daniel and Jennifer had moved to the couch, and Jennifer had stared at the floor as Daniel listened to Grandma talk through her shock.

Jennifer had woken up the next morning to find that someone had covered her with an afghan. Grandma and Daniel were sitting at the kitchen table again, drinking coffee, and Jennifer had been too preoccupied or in shock to ask if either of them had slept.

More and more, she thought less and less of her eighteen-year-old self.

"Mama Tyne called me," Daniel said quietly.

Jennifer snapped back to the present, and when she looked at Daniel looking at her, she felt a pang of guilt. "I could always count on you. If I needed you."

"That's me," he said ruefully. "Old reliable."

"That's not what I meant."

"But that's how it was," he said.

"I didn't expect you to still be waiting on me when I got back here, you know."

"Well, that's a good thing, for both our sakes." He didn't say it unkindly; he just stated it as fact.

She wanted to tell him she didn't think so, but it wasn't her right to say something like that. She wasn't even sure she agreed with herself. She glanced over the pictures again, but if there had been something there that she should have noticed, she couldn't find it now.

She stacked the photos of her mother's crime scene and put the stack aside, then pulled out the second bunch of paperwork.

It was Jonah. Her own birthday was the first thing she saw; it jumped out at her from the information sheet. She blinked a few times, then straightened up.

"Might as well get the worst of it over with," she said, and pulled the photos of the scene from the back.

She'd seen it all before, though the elderly fisherman who had stayed to comfort the two girls, while his son raced to town to get the police, had not let either one of them get close to the car again. She felt sorry for that old man, now. He'd been out fishing with his son, and they'd heard the shots. A middle-aged couple had come, too, but Jennifer really only remembered the old man.

Since the fisherman had tried to shield the girls, Jennifer saw for the first time the damage the bullet had done when it had come out through Jonah's throat. She knew from Inez that her brother had bolted upright when the first two shots were fired. One shattered the windshield. The second one hit Ned in the back of the head. One of the bullets that followed went through her brother's neck. That one, she knew from hearing her mother told, had been from a .30 caliber round, a rifle.

She spread the next few pictures out a bit, whether she was trying to get it over with faster, or whether she was just torturing herself, she didn't know. The second wound to her brother, which she knew about later but hadn't noticed at the time. Another bullet, this one a .38, had hit him in the back, just below his right shoulder. She blinked a few times and cleared her throat. The pictures were horrible, but they weren't any more horrible than being there, and she had been there.

It took her one moment too long to remember that Daniel hadn't, and she jerked her head up and looked at him.

He was sitting there, still as stone, staring at his best friend's torn throat, at the shot of him laid out on the ground, staring up at nothing ever again. Daniel sat there and stared, eyes wide and stricken, and Jennifer fought the immediate and overwhelming urge to comfort him.

"I'm so sorry," she said. "I wasn't thinking." She dropped her eyes and started gathering the photos, afraid she'd cry if she had to keep seeing that shattered look in his eyes.

She quickly gathered the photographs into a pile and shoved them back into the accordion file. Then she stared at the file for a long moment, and there was only the noise of the crickets and frogs coming through the window screen. Somewhere in there, she swore she could hear the sound of pain.

When she finally had the nerve to look at Daniel again, he was staring at her. She swallowed hard, trying to think of something appropriate to say that wouldn't embarrass either one of them. He saved her the trouble.

"That night..." His voice was sandpapery, and he cleared his throat. "When we were in your room. After you fell asleep, I...there was some blood you missed, behind your ear."

Jennifer felt a warm, swirling sensation in her stomach. She and Inez had been sent home from the hospital late in the evening, Inez with four stitches in her temple from broken glass and a bandage on her shoulder, where she'd been grazed by a bullet. Pastor Huddleston had driven Grandma and Mom home. Daniel had followed in his truck with Jennifer.

Later, after she'd taken a shower, she had fallen asleep on Daniel's chest. They were both in her room, fully-clothed and with the door open. She'd fallen asleep listening to Daniel's breathing over a gentle, mournful rain. She'd also heard the muffled sounds of her mother's cries, and Pastor Huddleston's gentle voice from the kitchen.

She could almost hear them now, as she sat there looking at Daniel. She could smell the greasy cotton of his work shirt from the gas station. The only reason he hadn't been at the lake that day was that he'd picked up an extra shift.

"I licked my thumb and wiped it off," Daniel said. "And I remember wondering—I still wonder sometimes—whose blood it was; Inez's, Jonah's, Ned's."

"I never touched Ned," she said quietly. "At least, I don't remember getting close...I don't know."

She studied Daniel's face, as memories she could smell and feel and taste washed over and through her. Lying on Daniel's chest, listening to his breath and his heartbeat and the rain. Feeling hot and chilled both, her hair still wet from her shower. She and Daniel had been alone in her bedroom more than once, though, as far as she remembered, always when someone else was home. Even so, they had come close, more than once, to becoming intimate. It was usually Jonah clearing his throat in the hallway, or the loud creak of the loose plank in front of Grandma's bedroom door that nipped it in the bud.

But as she sat there now, she realized nothing had ever been as intimate as lying on top of him, fully dressed in pajamas and a flannel robe. Neither of them speaking a word, as he lay there underneath her like a sponge, absorbing her grief and fear like it was spilled wine.

She felt the intimacy of it now, and felt her face color from the quiet between them then and the quiet between them now. That night eleven years ago, she could not have imagined a life without Daniel. Before the month was out, she'd been gone.

Jennifer realized they were still staring, and the look on his face made her wonder if they were remembering the same thing.

"You don't have to be here while I'm looking through this stuff," she said. "I'll be okay."

Daniel turned his glass around and around in the small pool of condensation that had formed beneath his tea. "You're not the only one who thinks about it, you know." He looked up at her. "I think about it all the time."

When Daniel left two hours later, it was full dark, and Jennifer felt drained and slightly sick. By the expression on Daniel's face when he'd said goodnight, he'd felt the same.

They'd spent the evening poring over photographs of dead bodies that had belonged to people they'd both loved. Gone over every detail of what the things that had killed them had done to their bodies. As police officers, they'd put themselves into the case materials hoping, but not admitting their hope, that they could solve the murders eleven years later. As the people left grieving, they wished someone had already done it.

CHAPTER 12

The next day was Friday, and if the weather just after sunrise was any indication, the weekend would be relentlessly hot and maliciously muggy. Anyone with plans for being outside over the weekend would probably gladly cancel them in exchange for a good thunderstorm.

By the time Jennifer sat down at her desk for the morning muster, she felt like she needed another shower. She and Daniel exchanged glances across the room when he came in, but other than that, she usually tried not to look at him too much when they were at the station. She didn't want the other guys wondering if they were together again, or if she was there just to see him, or whatever idiotic thing some of them might think. She didn't want Daniel embarrassed.

"Hey, Jennifer, check it out," Anthony said as he materialized at his desk. He held up a thin package with a clear plastic front. An impossibly-tiny onesie with *Sigmund & The Sea Monsters* on the front, and a matching pair of cloth booties. He held a paper cup of steaming coffee in the other hand.

"Oh, my gosh," Jennifer said, smiling.

"Leeanne at the diner gave it to us," Anthony said. "It can go either way, don't you think? Boy or girl?"

"I think so."

He put the box down on his desk, took a sip of his coffee, then set it down. "Listen, Nate Palmer called me this morning. I just got done telling the Chief."

Nate Palmer was a young black man who lived on Royal Street near downtown. He had two siblings in high school, and had been passing information along to Anthony about three men on his street who were supplying pot to junior high and high school kids and having them sell to other kids. Nate's little sister, Annie, was one of those school-aged dealers. She was fifteen years old. Ray and the district attorney had agreed that, in exchange for Nate's help in busting the three men, Annie would not go to jail.

Anthony had been working the case since about a week before Jennifer had come home. They knew that the guys were growing the pot somewhere outside of town, and distributing it from the house, but they had been waiting to know that there was a large enough amount of weed in the house to make a bust really worthwhile. Nobody wanted the guys back out on the street a week later because they'd only had a nickel bag on them.

"What's going on?" Jennifer asked. She took a big swallow of her own coffee. Maybe she was going to need it.

"Nate says Annie told him the kids are supposed to pick up fresh weed after school. Instead of watching *The Electric Company*, these kids are gonna be picking up dime bags."

"I don't think junior high and high school kids watch *The Electric Company*."

"Okay, *Dinah Shore*, whatever. Don't bust my chops this early in the morning."

"Aren't these guys going to know Nate's sister turned them in?" Jennifer asked.

Anthony shook his head. "There are four kids under sixteen working for these turkeys. We're gonna try to bust these guys before any of the kids get out of school." He shrugged. "If somebody skips school to go get their merchandise, we're gonna have to charge them, but anyone under sixteen is getting probation and community service, so Nate's sister isn't gonna stand out. The three kids that are over sixteen would get the whole nine yards if they're unlucky enough to be there."

"Fair, but not fair at the same time," Jennifer said.

Anthony shrugged. "Yeah, but the higher ups want this pot out of the schools. At least, the dealing. There's always gonna be kids with joints in their socks."

"So, what's the plan?"

"Chief's waking up the DA," Anthony answered. "He'll let us know at the muster."

Jennifer nodded. "Hey, tell Michelle I really enjoyed dinner, okay?"

"You told her that last night."

"Just tell her, would you?" Jennifer shook her head. "It was nice."

It had been nice. Anthony and his wife had a modest home, but it had been warm and inviting, like Michelle. Jennifer had liked her immediately. She was cute without trying, and although she was quiet, she had a sharp wit and an easy and unself-conscious laugh.

"Nobody makes Johnny Mozzetti like Michelle," Anthony said. "She had a nice time, too. We haven't been having much company lately 'cause she gets tired pretty easily these days."

Just then, Ray walked into the room from his office and clapped his hands a few times. "All right, people, let's get it together. We got a busy day ahead."

Three hours later, Jennifer squatted behind a misshapen, aluminum garden shed in Morris Graves' back yard. Like most of the guys, she'd left her officer's cap back in the patrol car. All of that thick, black cotton and rigid plastic trapped the heat between a cop's scalp and the cap itself. The visor had nothing in the brim to protect an officer from the line of sweat that appeared there almost immediately, and the heat rash that followed it in what seemed like minutes.

Yes, it would have been nice to have something to keep the sweat out of the eyes, but the cap *caused* so much more sweat than going bareheaded, that there really wasn't much to recommend the wearing of it on a July day.

Jennifer had been in that position, under the white-hot, late morning sun, for almost an hour. She'd been squinting across the yard all that time, her eyes moving between the dusty jalousies of the back door and Patterson, who was similarly squatting at the east back corner of the house, but facing the side and front yards. He was waiting on a radio signal from Ray, who was parked two blocks north in a Southern Bell van. Two officers were also stationed in an old pickup at the east end. They had been waiting on a maroon Nova driven by a light-skinned man with a large afro, and supposedly delivering several pounds of pot. Once the man arrived, the officers at the Graves house would be put on alert. They would move in once the delivery man, and the goods he was delivering, were inside the house.

Jennifer felt a rivulet of sweat trickle down her spine and underneath the waistband of her pants. She was almost vibrating with the need to untuck her shirt and swipe at it. The bulletproof vest she wore, one of several recently acquired by the Dismal PD, was heavy, stiff and cumbersome, and allowed no ventilation at all. Morris Graves and his associates had no registered weapons, and none reported by anecdote, either. None of them had ever been violent other than Graves being charged in a bar fight. But, men in this line of work frequently owned unregistered weapons, and it was safest to assume they'd use them if they panicked.

Though she couldn't see him, she knew that Daniel was in the bushes of an abandoned house next door, toward the front of the yard. He and Whitney were supposed to go through the front door, followed quickly by Ray and the other guys parked on the street. Patterson, Anthony and Jennifer had the back door. Jennifer could hear Anthony breathing occasionally, from his post on the other side of the shed.

Annie had told her brother that most of the business was conducted in the dining room at the back, west corner of the house, which had a large window overlooking the back yard. The window had brown curtains pulled shut, but they'd thought it best not to try to take positions at the back door, which would necessitate them having to cross the mostly-bare yard.

Jennifer was blinking sweat out of her eyes when she saw Patterson raise his hand. The first signal, meaning the maroon Nova had turned onto Royal Street. The second signal would mean that the delivery guy and his goods were inside the house, and that Ray and the other men parked on the street were moving in fast.

Jennifer stared at Patterson's upraised hand, afraid to blink unless absolutely necessary. What felt like maybe two minutes later, Patterson dropped his hand and started a crouching run toward the back door. Anthony beat Jennifer into the open back yard, but only by a few steps.

Jennifer had only been part of two similar busts. They were all scary, with so many known and unknown variables that it was impossible to fully prepare the mind for what would happen. Instead, she prepared her mind in terms of a resolute decision to do what had to be done, regardless of how it looked like it might turn out.

As she had found on the other two busts, long periods of waiting and a mental girding of the loins turned instantly into an almost slow-motion series of events, like a home movie someone had cut up and then pasted back together.

The adrenaline spike was instantaneous, and the heat, sweat, cramping muscles and almost every other physical sensation faded, while the details of the scene and everyone's actions came into sharp focus.

She heard a commotion, and the sound of men's raised voices from inside the house just before Patterson reached the back steps. He never got to the back door. It was flung open, and a burly man in his early twenties, wearing brown checked bell bottoms and a *Fat Albert* T-shirt, came roaring down the three steps. Patterson almost stopped him, but the man let out a growl and clotheslined Patterson in the chest, knocking him into a stumble. Anthony was there almost immediately, helping Patterson to wrestle the man to the ground. Jennifer was continuing toward the back door when a tall, skinny man in a slouchy hat came flying out, barreling past the clump of men on the ground and heading for the alley behind the house.

As she was changing her trajectory to follow, Jennifer saw Daniel in her peripheral vision, as he ran out the back door and jumped the steps, landing with a grunt.

Jennifer had a good fifteen yards on Daniel by the time he hit the grass, and the skinny man had at least thirty. Jennifer's legs were not only long but strong, and she would have caught up to the skinny man with ease if she hadn't been burdened by her twenty-pound gun belt and stiff, bulky vest.

The skinny man vaulted over the sagging chain link fence at the back and headed east down the alley. Jennifer ran over his slouchy hat before jumping onto and over the fence herself. Several strides down the dirt alley, she heard the jangle of the fence as Daniel followed. She could hear the man ahead breathing heavily with the effort of his flight. She could hear her own breath in her ears, and Daniel huffing behind her, like they were all in some airtight bubble together.

Several kids too young for school stopped their sandbox play in a yard across the alley as the skinny man passed. A heavyset black woman in pink curlers and bright blue shorts stood at her clothesline, holding up a sheet as she watched them with mild interest.

A few houses down on the right, an elderly woman with garden shears in her hand squinted after the skinny man. "Terrell White, what you done, boy?" she yelled angrily.

White veered to the left, into a smaller alley that led to the street. Jennifer did a two-second visual calculation and turned into the yard just before it. She could see flashes of White through the bushes that lined the yard. At first, he was ahead of her, then almost alongside. Jennifer pumped her legs harder than she thought she actually could, her chest screaming, and veered to the right as the bushes ended, coming into the alley inches behind White, who jerked his head to look at her, the whites of his eyes impossibly large.

Jennifer tackled him where the alley ended at a small patch of grass between two houses. White cushioned both their falls by pushing his face through the sod for a good twelve inches. Once they came to a stop, with Jennifer more or less lying on his back, Jennifer pulled her handcuffs from her belt. She was pulling Terrell White's left arm behind him, without resistance, when she heard Daniel's footfalls behind them, and he skidded to a stop.

"I got him!" he said breathlessly. He dropped to one knee and took White's left arm. He reached for the right as Jennifer lifted herself up, pressed a knee into White's back, and opened her cuffs.

"You honky mothers are killin' me, man!" White groaned. "I can't breathe!" His words were muffled somewhat by the dirt he was trying to spit out of his mouth.

Jennifer got the cuffs on him and stood, and Daniel helped White to his feet, then gently pushed him toward Jennifer. She grabbed the man's arm.

An older black man, with a running water hose in his hand, watched from his yard a dozen feet away. "About time they caught y'all ass, sellin' drugs to children," he said. "Shamin' your mother, God rest her."

White bent over to spit and snort more dirt from his mouth and nose, and Daniel looked over him at Jennifer. "What were you thinking, running off after him alone?" he hissed, which Jennifer was pretty sure he wouldn't have asked Patterson.

"That I can still outrun you," she snapped.

He looked at her for a moment. "Oh, I don't know. I seem to remember catching you once or twice," he said quietly.

Jennifer felt her face warm, and she hoped the flush of exertion covered it. She deflected by reading White his rights.

A few minutes later, they met Patterson in the alley behind Groves' house, as he was coming to find them. Behind him, the large man in the *Fat Albert* shirt sat in the yard with his beefy arms behind his back, as Ray and Anthony stood talking to him.

"Atta boy, Huddleston," Patterson said, smiling.

"I didn't catch him, she did," Daniel answered as he passed him.

"Sure, she did." Patterson smirked at Jennifer.

Jennifer stopped and scowled at him.

"You think he caught him *for* me, like blowing a bubble in my gum before giving it back to me?"

"Save it, Jennifer," Daniel called back.

"I'm so tired of your crap, Patterson," Jennifer said. "Why don't you go see who set the record for the 200- *and* the 400-yard dash two years in a row."

Daniel stopped and looked back at them. "Still a record."

"Still?" Jennifer asked, surprised.

"Hey, I almost beat that record on the 200-yard dash, my junior year," White mentioned.

"Yeah, well, almost didn't count today, either," Daniel said. He looked at Patterson. "You know what sucks about you hating her so damn much just because she's a woman?"

Patterson put his hands on his hips. "No, what?"

"If you actually knew her, you'd probably like her." Daniel kept walking.

"I doubt that," Patterson answered, as he fell into step beside Jennifer. "And for the record, I don't hate her, I hate her being a cop. I hate that I'm probably going to have to depend on her at some point to watch my back."

"She's standing right here," Jennifer muttered. "And you just did."

Late that afternoon, everyone that was in the station was either packing up to leave, finishing up their work, or chatting with the incoming night shift. Anthony had already gone home, and Jennifer finished putting away their carbon copies of their arrest reports, then tossed her empty coffee cup into the trash can beside her desk.

She grabbed her keys, found the tiny brass key that went to her lap drawer, and locked it. Wednesday, Patterson or Whitney or one of the other guys had left an empty birth control compact in her desk. She had no idea where they'd gotten it, but she'd started locking her desk. She wasn't afraid of the guys who were picking on her, or of what they might leave in her desk, but she hated the idea that they would invade her personal workspace that way.

She had to jimmy the key to get it out of the scratched-up old lock, and she was doing that when the hairs on her forearms went up and her eyes squinted of their own accord. She stared at the key in her hand, and at the lock on her drawer, waiting for one of them to explain themselves.

"Now what?" Daniel asked from beside her.

She jerked her head up. She hadn't seen him coming. "Nothing."

She looked back down at the lock, and then felt a warm swirling in her stomach. She saw her mother's body, in black and white. Saw the inside of her car. Then she saw it all in color, like she'd been dropped right back into 1962.

"Jen."

She looked back up at him. "Mom's car door."

"What?"

"The other night, when we were looking at the pictures, there was something, but then we were talking and I couldn't figure out what it was. It was her passenger door. It was unlocked."

"So?"

"She always locked it as soon as she got in the car. I can see her doing it. She'd lean over the passenger seat and push down the lock, or if I was in the car, she'd tell me to do it right away."

Daniel frowned. "But there were cops all over that car," he said. "I don't doubt that one of them unlocked it from your Mom's side to let another cop in."

"Before the crime scene photos were taken?" Jennifer asked. "Would you do that?"

He blinked a couple of times. "No. But the picture you're talking about could have been taken after they already had enough pictures of the scene as it was." He held up a hand. "I know, I just thought the same thing; the keys were still in the ignition in those pictures. What cop would lean across a body to unlock the door?"

"I need to talk to Ray," Jennifer said.

Jennifer headed for Ray's office, and she heard Daniel follow. Ray's door was open, and she knocked on the jamb. He looked up and waved her in, his face registering a moment's surprise when he saw Daniel come in behind her.

"What's up?" he asked.

"Ray, were you at the scene—Mom's scene—the night it happened?"

It took him a second to catch up. He'd obviously expected them to be there about something work-related, in the present day.

"No, I was working that night, but I wasn't allowed anywhere near the scene or the case. Why?"

Jennifer glanced over at Daniel before answering. "In the pictures, of her body in the car, her passenger door is unlocked."

Ray frowned at her. "I don't understand the significance of that."

"Do you remember that time somebody threw a dead bird through her passenger window when she was at a red light? She was always really careful after that. She always locked both her car doors as soon as she got in. She was even more careful after Jonah."

Ray sat back, and the creaking of his chair seemed loud in the suddenly quiet office. He stared at something past her, maybe something in the past altogether. After a moment, he looked back at Jennifer.

"The prevailing theory was that someone was waiting for her at the shop," he said. "That they attacked her as she was getting out of her car. If I'm following you here, you're suggesting either she unlocked the car door for somebody who was there, or maybe someone was in the car with her."

Jennifer nodded slightly. "Yes."

He rubbed at his jaw. "Someone she knew."

"Someone she trusted," Jennifer clarified. "Mom was really paranoid after Jonah, even though I don't think she thought it was connected to her. Maybe she did and didn't talk about it in front of me, but..."

Ray shook his head. "Until Claire was killed, nobody really thought what happened at the lake had anything to do with her. Race? Yes. It was only a month after desegregation here. Tension was high, tempers were flaring; it was a hard time. But nobody connected the lake murders to Claire's activism until she was killed, too."

"I remember that a lot of people thought she deserved to lose her son because of it." Jennifer said it quietly, but with a bitter edge to her words. "That he was shot because he was with a colored girl and Mom deserved that because of what she was doing for colored people."

Ray ran a hand through his hair and sighed. "Yeah, there were idiots who said things like that. But let me explain something you might not have noticed, or might not remember. There were a lot of people in this town, white people, who supported your mother. Some openly, some not. There were just as many white folks at your mother's funeral as there were black, and you shouldn't forget that."

Tears sprang to Jennifer's eyes from nowhere, and she blinked. "No. You're right, I shouldn't. I do forget that sometimes."

"I'm not reprimanding you, Jennifer," Ray said. "I just want you to remember that there are good *and* bad people in this town, and they're both black *and* white."

He leaned back again and sighed. Jennifer had almost forgotten Daniel was beside her until he spoke.

"You probably knew or remember the adults in her life better than us. Besides all of us, you have any idea who Jennifer's mom might have let in her car?"

Ray looked at him a moment. "What are *you* doing?"

Daniel looked uncomfortable for just a second, then straightened his spine. "Look, I wasn't exactly excited that Jen's looking into this case—"

"Reading it, not looking into it," Ray said sternly.

"Reading it, then," Daniel said. "But since she is, I want to know what happened, too."

Ray pointed at Jennifer. "Shut the door."

Jennifer walked to the open door. Patterson squinted at her curiously from his desk, and a couple of night shift cops who were walking by glanced at her and Daniel both as they passed. Jennifer shut the door quietly and walked back to the desk.

"Great. Now they'll all think Daniel and I are asking permission to date again or something."

"That's better than them thinking you guys are trying to do a better job on a case that was investigated by two of their fellow officers."

"I've never thought that Murray and—what's the other—"

"Frank Hamilton," Daniel said.

"Hamilton. I never suggested they didn't do a good job," Jennifer said. "And I'm not suggesting it now, either. They had no reason to think anything of the fact that her passenger door was unlocked."

"No, they didn't," Ray said. "I've pored over that case myself a few times over the years, and I didn't notice it, and it wouldn't have meant anything to me if I had. I don't even remember the last time I was in a car with your mom."

"I saw that they interviewed my father and checked his alibi," Jennifer said. "Was that just because they were divorced?"

"That's right. Always check the spouse first," Ray answered. "A few people remembered him being over at Monty's that night, but nobody remembered for sure when he left. The house is only a couple of blocks away from the bar, and he was passed out drunk when Murray and Hamilton went over there around midnight. He wasn't much of a suspect, anyway. He told plenty of people that she was right to leave him. He was angry for a while, but he got over it years before your mom was killed. Besides, there was the lake, and a definite racial connection. And Willie lost *his* son, too."

"Okay," Jennifer said. "I just wanted to make sure."

"Listen, I know they fought sometimes when they were married, and I couldn't stand the guy from the get-go, but he went to hell in a handbasket when Jonah was killed. After Claire, he was a goner. I don't think he'll ever climb out of that bottle. He ever contact you out there in New Orleans?"

"He didn't know where I was," Jennifer answered. "I don't even know if he asked."

Ray sighed and stood up. "Listen, I know you want answers. We all do. The door lock is meaningful, but it's not enough for us to get the go-ahead to reopen the case. If you find something in that file that's more concrete, then I'll go to the D.A. But until then, you don't talk to people about it, you don't go around poking sticks into copperhead nests, nothing. You get me?"

He looked at each of them until they'd nodded in turn.

"I'm not brushing you off, Jennifer. If you think of something that can actually lead us to these guys, we'll go after them," he said, and his eyes darkened. "Although it would be in their best interests to already be dead."

CHAPTER 13

Saturday was bright and hot, with possible thunderstorms late in the day, but nothing to bring relief at high noon, when Inez and Jennifer set out for Ebby's Market.

They'd spent the last couple of hours supervising a gaggle of Tyne kids and Inez's two little ones as they took turns on the Slip n' Slide in the back yard. Now Mama Tyne was getting the youngest kids fed and down for naps, and she'd had "a taste" for a cold Coca-Cola, which they didn't keep in the house.

Inez had tied a white button-down shirt over her bathing suit top and pulled on some cut-offs, and Jennifer had changed back into her T-shirt and shorts. Their flip-flops flip-flopped over the uneven sidewalk as they walked the four blocks to the store.

Everyone was outside, despite the heat. Old women sat together on aluminum chairs in the front yard or in rockers on the porch, fanning themselves with magazines, or paper fans they'd gotten at church. Old men hung over shared fences or dug in their flowerbeds. One group of kids played kickball in an empty lot, another played hopscotch in somebody's driveway.

Young women sat with babies in the grass while little ones played in the sprinklers. Young men worked on their cars, mowed the grass, or gathered in little clusters, listening to somebody's car radio. Most everyone they passed made note of Jennifer; even now, a white woman was a rare sight in this neighborhood. Some waved or said hello, some glared, others just went back to their conversations.

Just as in 1962, or 1957, or any other time in Jennifer's memory, there were several people hanging out in pairs or groups in front of Ebby's. Thirteen- and fourteen-year-old girls with picks sticking out of their hair blew bubbles and tried not to look self-conscious. Young men congregated in patches around the small parking lot, smoking cigarettes and drinking sodas. Five blocks away, the young men standing outside Floyd's Package Store were drinking cold beers out of paper bags, but Ebby's didn't sell alcohol, or allow it on the premises.

A group of three men leaned on the chest that held bags of ice, and they stared at Inez and Jennifer as they approached the front door.

"Oh, Christy Love!" said a man in old work trousers and a white button-down shirt that hung open over his undershirt. "Girl, you are looking fine today. Let's you and me go somewhere a while."

"Get lost, Turner," Inez said, without actually being unfriendly. "You know I've got a real man."

"Well, maybe your lovely friend here would like to take a walk off Honky Street," he said, smiling.

"She doesn't need some jive turkey with a roach clip in his hair," Inez said, opening the front door. Jennifer couldn't help laughing softly.

"Oooh, burn!" one of Turner's friends said.

"I can smell the scorch comin' off the brother's skin," said the other one, but all three of them were laughing.

Jennifer was greeted with the familiar smells of Pine-Sol, coffee, hamburgers and vinegar, all being blown around the store by the box fans in every window. She was amazed to see Ebenezer Jackson himself behind the counter. He had to be eighty years old, and his hair had gone completely white. A middle-aged man Jennifer didn't recognize worked at a stove and flat-top grill a little further down.

There were several rows of metal shelves and wire racks on the left side of the store, and coolers and a few tables in back. A few men who were clearly on breaks from work were sitting down to a quick lunch.

On the right was a long, glass display case. Inside were pans of fried chicken, greens and devilled eggs. On the top of the case were giant jars of pickled eggs, pickled sausage, garlic pickles, and beef jerky, each one accompanied by a coffee cup with a pair of tongs in it. When they were kids, Jennifer had eaten her weight in those pickled eggs.

"Hey, Mr. Ebby," Inez said with a big smile.

"Hey yourself, Inez," he said back, a gold tooth glinting from his own smile. "Who this, then?"

"This is my best friend, Jen. You remember her."

Jennifer smiled at the old man as he squinted at her. "Well, my law, so it is, too!" he said.

"How are you, Mr. Ebby?" Jennifer asked.

"Just fine, just fine," the old man answered. He handed a package wrapped in white butcher paper to the middle-aged woman waiting at the counter. "Here you go, Miss Diane."

"I'm gonna go get Mama's Coca-Cola and grab a couple treats for the kids," Inez said. "What do you want?"

"Just a Coke."

Inez headed toward the other side of the store, and Jennifer turned back to Mr. Ebby.

"You been gone a long while," he was saying. "Long time. I was sorry to hear Mrs. Quindlen passed; God rest her."

"Thank you." Jennifer decided to have a pickled egg after all, and grabbed a napkin from a metal dispenser.

"What a good woman she was. Funny lady, oh my law she was funny."

Jennifer smiled as she opened the jar. "She was."

"You here to see to the house, then?"

"I'm home for good," she answered, choosing her egg and putting it in her napkin.

"Now, that's good. That would please her, I think."

"I think so." Jen screwed the lid back on the jar. On the little portable TV behind the counter, a baseball game played in black and white. Someone must have hit a good one, because people were jumping from their seats and she could just make out the excited voice of the announcer.

"Isn't it a shame what we do, one to another?" Mr. Ebby was saying, shaking his head. "Breakin' the heart of the Lord."

Jennifer was pretty sure she didn't need to ask what he was talking about. "Yes, sir," she replied quietly.

"It's good that you come on home, chile. Good, though."

Inez walked up to Jennifer with the necks of three bottles of Coke in one hand and a fistful of treats in the other. There were two, foot-long sticks of Bub's Daddy bubble gum, one grape and one green apple, a Sugar Daddy, and two Charms Pops.

"Look at this, then," Mr. Ebby said, laughing. "Mutt and Jeff back in here after all these years, with their pickled eggs and their Co-Colas and candy, just like always."

"Now, Mr. Ebby, you know this candy ain't for me," Inez said.

"That the truth, then?" He nodded. "Who's gonna eat that Sugar Daddy?"

"You know what, Mr. Ebby?" She dumped the booty on the counter. "Some people drink or smoke weed. I eat like two of these a month. Go on, now."

"Ever' Saturday's when you eat a Sugar Daddy," he said back.

Inez was going to reply when she saw Jennifer pull a five out of her back pocket. "No, uh-uh. I brought money."

"Just let me get it, Inez. It's not like I'm out blowing my paycheck every week."

"I know that's right," her friend replied. "We need to get you out, get you some new clothes or go to the movies or something."

"That would be good."

Jennifer had fallen asleep in Grandma's recliner the night before, the case file at her feet and Johnny Carson on TV.

"You girls have a good day, now," Mr. Ebby said as he handed Jennifer her change.

"You, too, Mr. Ebby," Jennifer said.

"You too, sir." Inez took the little paper bag and one of the Cokes. Jennifer popped the caps off the other ones, using the opener that was screwed to the side of the counter.

Jennifer handed Inez her soda, and they went back out into the scorching heat, blinking against the white brightness of the day. Turner and his friends whistled and said their goodbyes, and the two women drank their sodas as they headed back the way they'd come.

When they got back to the house, the older kids were watching *Soul Train* in the living room, Mama Tyne was washing up the lunch dishes, and Daniel was at the kitchen table, eating greens and a pork neck from a pink Tupperware bowl.

Inez dumped the candy on the kitchen table. "Hey, Daniel," she said with a smile. "What are you doing here?"

"Being obedient," he said as he stood.

"Look at him, looking like he doesn't have any food in his icebox," Mama Tyne said. "

Inez and Daniel hugged. A real hug, as opposed to a polite one. "How you doing?" she asked him.

"Good. How are you?"

"Good."

She looked over at Jennifer, like Jennifer had been hiding something. Jennifer ignored the look by taking the unopened Coke to Mama Tyne.

"Oh, thank you, baby," the woman said. "This is just what I need."

She turned to rummage through a utensil drawer, and Jennifer looked at Daniel, eyebrows raised. "What *are* you doing here?"

"You weren't home, so I drove by here and saw your car."

"Okay."

Daniel was sitting back down to his snack, and didn't look at her. "I got us an appointment with those guys we were talking about yesterday."

"What guys?"

He looked up at her as he picked up a pork neck. "About fixing your barn."

Inez looked over at Jennifer. "Why would you pay people to fix that barn? That's what the boys are for."

Inez's four brothers ranged in age from twenty-six to twenty, but Inez still referred to them as "the boys".

"It's okay," Jennifer said. "We're just…" She looked at Daniel. It was his lie, but he was chewing rather than helping. She looked back at Inez. "We're just gonna see if it's worth fixing or not."

Inez looked her suspiciously. She glanced at Daniel, then back at Jennifer. "That's the best you could do?"

Mama Tyne sank into a kitchen chair with her Coke in one hand and a banana in the other. "I told Daniel he needs to come by more often, especially now. We haven't seen him—except on the street—we haven't seen him since Anna passed."

Daniel smiled at her as he wiped his fingers on a paper napkin. Jennifer hadn't seen him smile that warmly since she'd been back. He always had loved Mama Tyne.

"I should come around and see you more," he said.

"You going to church?" she asked him.

He shrugged. "Most of the time."

"What's Pastor Huddleston say about that?"

"He says it's not too late for me to become a degenerate," Daniel said, grinning. He got up and took his bowl and fork to the trash can. "He's okay. He knows I'm working some things out."

He scraped his bones into the trash and put his bowl in the sink.

"Leave that; you got to be somewhere," Mama Tyne told him.

"I need to go home and change first," Jennifer said.

Daniel looked at her shorts. "Okay. Why don't I just wait for you at your house, then?"

Jennifer nodded. "Okay."

He hugged Mama Tyne and Inez in turn, and said his goodbyes, then Inez and Jennifer followed him to the door. Inez held the door open, and once Daniel was on his way to his truck, she grinned at Jennifer.

"I'll see you later," Jennifer said.

"Yeah, good luck with your barn," Inez said. "Tell the Amish guys I said hey."

CHAPTER 14

Daniel waited in his truck in the driveway, as Jennifer hurriedly changed into tan trousers and a light blue short-sleeved top. She pulled her hair out of a ponytail and swiped on some lip gloss, but she ignored the temptation to check her appearance more than once, or do anything more to enhance it. She and Daniel weren't on a date; they were going to talk to the two cops who had investigated both the lake murders and the murder of her mother.

Jennifer had intended to follow Daniel in her own car, but when he asked why she should bother using the extra gas, she didn't have a good reason, so she climbed in.

"We're going to see Kenneth Murray first," Daniel said as he turned around and headed down the driveway. "Do you remember him?"

"I remember two cops, but I don't know which is which," she answered. "There was a guy with reddish-brown hair and freckles—"

"That's Frank Hamilton."

"So Murray is the guy with the dark hair and receding hairline."

"It's done receding."

"I don't really have much of an impression of them, except that I was intimidated by them, and I felt like they asked me the same questions over and over."

"I'm sure they did. You were at both scenes."

"Yeah, I do remember *that*," Jennifer said quietly. She looked out the window as they drove away from town, further out Citrus Trail. "Does he live out in the sticks?"

"Not too far out. He's out there on Live Oak Road, where the little Negro Hospital was."

"I always thought that was strange," Jennifer said. "Most of the blacks around here live in town, but if they had an emergency, they had to go four or five miles outside the city limits."

"Yeah. It's a vet now."

"How well do you know Murray?" Jennifer asked, looking back over at Daniel.

"Not all that well. I mean, he just retired a couple of months ago, so obviously we've worked together here and there, but we were never partners or anything."

Jennifer had been away a long time, but she recognized that tone Daniel got when he was trying to be neutral or polite, but didn't actually feel that way.

"So, what don't you like about him?" she asked.

He glanced over at her, then looked back at the road and shrugged. "He's mouthy. Arrogant. He had thirty years in the department, so nobody could tell him anything."

"Was he a good cop?"

"Actually, he was. He was Messer's partner the last couple of years."

"He told me."

"Messer says he learned a lot from him. He just hated driving around with him in the patrol car."

Jennifer gave him half a grin. "Yeah, he told me that, too."

They were quiet for a couple of minutes. Jennifer stared at his hands on the steering wheel. It was weird; she had always liked Daniel's hands, and she had stared at them a lot when they were young. His fingers were long and slender, but his hands were strong. They had a little more hair on the knuckles now, a little more tan to the skin. But at the same time, she recognized every bone, every angle, every scar. It was as if she'd never stopped staring.

"He's not going to like you being there," Daniel said.

"No?" Not that she was surprised.

"He also doesn't know you're coming."

"What?" Jennifer snapped. Now she was.

He looked over at her. "He doesn't even know why *I'm* coming out there. I just told him I needed to talk to him about something. Of course, he knows you're in town, and he most certainly knows you're a cop—they had that little thing in the paper last week about the first female police officer—and he still goes into Monty's and hangs out with some of the guys."

Jennifer shook her head slowly as Daniel shrugged.

"And then, you know, of course he remembers that we were together," Daniel added.

"I can't believe you didn't tell him I was coming!"

"Well, he wouldn't have told me to come out there if I had, Jen!"

Daniel turned back to the road as a tan station wagon with kids, a dog and an inner tube in the back passed them going the other way.

"Why not? He was my twin brother. She was my mom," Jennifer insisted.

"Well, for one thing, he doesn't like women," Daniel snapped. "Unless they're lying down, quietly. And I just got done telling you he's arrogant, especially about his prowess as a cop. You think he's going to take it well that a woman cop, the teenybopper from eleven years ago, is going to come ask him questions about his biggest case? His *unsolved* case?"

"I don't care what he thinks."

Daniel huffed out a laugh that pegged her as an idiot. "Yes, you do, if you want him to talk to us."

"Do you think he's going to love being surprised?" she asked drily.

"Well, we'll find out in less than a minute, 'cause there's our turn," Daniel said. "So maybe we should calm down and regulate our breathing so he doesn't think we were making out in the truck."

Live Oak Road only had a few houses on it, most of them with five or ten acres of property, and most of the homes were old cabins or shotgun cottages, so Jennifer was surprised to find that Kenneth Murray's house looked new.

It was a log house, one-and-a-half stories, with a front porch that spanned the width of the house. It was set back from the road, with a U-shaped gravel driveway. Parked there was a blue Chevy pickup that looked to be just a few years old. There was a load of sod piled in back.

The lot around the house was largely wooded, mostly with loblolly and slash pines, some of them fifty or sixty feet tall. To the left of the cabin was a timber machine shed, with a small sawmill inside.

"This isn't what I expected," Jennifer said as they made their way up the driveway.

"He built it himself. He rented a duplex over on Fifth Street for the longest time, but he came out here weekends for…I don't know, five years or something like that. Building his retirement cabin."

The front door opened as Daniel parked behind Murray's truck and shut off his engine. Once she saw him, Jennifer remembered him better than she thought she had. He was maybe an inch or two over Daniel's six-one, a tall man who was starting to go to seed around the middle. He wore khaki trousers and a white T-shirt that clung somewhat to the paunch above his waistband.

He stared right at Jennifer as Daniel got out of the truck, and he had a slight smile on his face that didn't really make him look friendly. He had one hand on the door and held a can of Schlitz in the other.

Jennifer was about to open her door when Daniel beat her to it. She got out and followed him down a short gravel path to the front steps made of three halved logs.

"Hey, Murray," Daniel said as they started up the steps.

"Well, hello there, Daniel," Murray said, but he was looking at Jennifer. "Hello, *Ms.* Sheehan. I'm sorry, Officer Sheehan, come to bring the ERA to Dismal, Florida."

"You're unhappy about her coming," Daniel said. "I—"

"I have no feelings one way or the other about her being here," Murray interrupted mildly. "But I would have expected *you* to be more upfront about it."

"I thought it would be better if you met before you told me 'no', Daniel said.

"But we have met," Murray said, finally looking at Daniel. He stepped back. "Come on in."

Daniel let Jennifer go first, and when she stepped inside, she was surprised to find it was at least twenty degrees cooler in the house. The second floor covered only the back of the house, and the ceilings in the main room were two stories tall. Two long ceiling fans spun slowly from the rafters. The living area was just inside the door, and arranged around a rough fieldstone fireplace. At the far end of the room was a galley kitchen with a bar separating it from the living room.

Murray closed the door, then led them toward the kitchen. A large coffee table was covered with boating magazines and TV Guides, a large, amber glass ashtray that was empty but dirty, and a wooden duck decoy. There was a console television/stereo near the fireplace, and a record was playing. The volume was low, but high enough that she heard Roger Miller singing "King of the Road."

On the walls were several animal heads and a few photographs of Murray with various men, sometimes in hunting gear and other times in light pants and polo shirts, sitting or standing in the cockpit of a fishing boat. The pictures were taken somewhere on or off the coast. He saw her looking at one that was hung near the kitchen bar.

"*The Right Miranda*," he said, smiling. "A little cop humor. I got her in '66. I keep her over in Destin." He walked around the bright yellow Formica bar. "Have a seat."

Jennifer and Daniel each sat in one of the yellow bar stools with lattice backs and brown vinyl seat cushions.

Murray held up his beer. "Obviously, I have Schlitz. And obviously, you're not on duty. But I also have Tab, orange juice and tea."

"I'll take some tea, thanks," Daniel said.

Murray looked at Jennifer. "Tab's fine," she said, though she hated Tab.

"This is really nice," Daniel said, looking around as Murray opened the fridge.

"You've never been out here?"

"No."

Jennifer didn't know whether that fact was meant to insult Daniel, or if actually meant nothing at all.

"Lot of the guys helped out now and then when I was building the place," Murray said.

He popped the Tab open and set it in front of Jennifer, then grabbed a pitcher of tea from the fridge and a glass from the dish rack.

"So, what can I do for the two of you?" Murray asked, his back to them as he poured the tea.

Jennifer beat Daniel to the punch. "We won't take too much of your time. I just wanted to ask you a couple of questions about my mother."

Murray turned and set Daniel's tea down in front of him. "You mean your mother's case, I assume, since I didn't actually know your mother."

"Yes."

"Ask away." The light from the brown woven swag lamp over the bar reflected off his bald head. The remaining hair on the sides and in the back was neatly trimmed and still dark.

"I was looking at the pictures from the scene," Jennifer said.

"Why would you want to do that?"

"Because I was an eighteen-year-old girl at the time. Now I'm almost thirty, and a police officer. I thought I might be able to understand everything better now than I did then."

"All right."

Out of the corner of her eye, Jennifer saw Daniel take a sip of his tea. "In the pictures, the ones before my mother's body was removed, the passenger side door was unlocked."

"And her door was wide open," Murray said. "Why does the other door matter?"

"Because my mother was bordering on paranoid *before* my brother and Ned were killed," Jennifer answered. "She always pushed that lock down before she even got in the car. Or had me or Jonah do it, if we were with her."

Murray looked at her thoughtfully, then took a drink of his beer. "Your mother was distraught after your brother's murder. Maybe she forgot."

Jennifer shook her head slowly. "No. I rode with her or drove her somewhere several times after my brother was killed. She never forgot."

"Jennifer's pretty certain that her Mom was even more careful after the lake," Daniel said. "Even if she had no idea that her family was being targeted. The whole town was charged up after the murders."

"I remember," Murray said flatly. He finished his beer and tossed it into a trash can by the fridge. Then he leaned back against the sink. "We didn't have any way of knowing she kept that door locked," he said to Jennifer.

"I know you didn't. I'm not saying you should have. I would have told you, but I didn't even notice it that night. I just wanted to know if maybe someone at the scene had unlocked it."

"Young lady, I was a police officer for thirty years," he said slowly, folding his arms across his chest. "Decorated. I know how to behave at a murder scene."

Jennifer breathed in through her nose, trying not to show it. It wouldn't do her any good to smart off and make him mad. "I didn't mean you, Sgt. Murray," she said, tacking on the "Sgt." to soothe him. "But maybe a younger officer, somebody new. Or one of the ambulance people."

"Frank and I were working a robbery case together when we got the call," he said. "We were the first ones at the scene. You were in the car with the colored woman—"

"Mrs. Tyne," Jennifer interjected.

He just nodded. "Frank checked your mother for a pulse—not because he needed to, but because he was required to—and not one other person got anywhere near that car until I was finished taking those pictures."

It seemed strange to Jennifer, to be here looking at the man who took the photographs she'd been staring at for days. To be in his house.

"Okay," she said.

She took a sip of the Tab she didn't want, to hide her nervousness and disappointment. She hadn't realized it until just then, but she'd been hoping some patrolman fresh from the academy had unlocked that car door.

Murray opened the fridge again. Jennifer had expected him to grab another beer, but he had a little carafe of orange juice instead, one of those ones with the oranges painted on it. He got another glass from the drainer and filled it halfway. Then he leaned back against the counter and took a drink before he spoke again.

"So, if I'm interpreting your face correctly, you're wondering if someone had been in the car with her, or if someone she knew had been waiting for her and she unlocked the other door for him for whatever reason."

"Yes."

He took another sip of his juice, then looked thoughtfully at the floor. "The assumption was, since she was alone when she left the Food Fair earlier, and no one was around downtown to see her pull into her shop, that somebody had been waiting for her, maybe behind that half wall that separated her lot from the house behind it. Maybe behind the trash cans."

He looked up at Jennifer. "What it looked like to us, is that she was getting out of the car and somebody came up on her. She was only parked about ten feet from the back door."

"That made sense to me, too," Jennifer said. "She knew we were on our way. A couple of volunteers were going to be there soon, too."

"Making posters for that rally up in Dothan."

"Yes."

Claire had set up an office of sorts on the second floor of her dress shop. Various volunteers met there to plan, to talk, to stuff envelopes or make posters or print up petitions. Lots of people knew about it, and lots of people had known that she and some of the volunteers would be there that night. There had always been a bit of theorizing, even before Claire's murder, that one of the white volunteers was actually a "spy".

Daniel spoke up. "We've always assumed that, even if the people who killed Ned and Jonah and Claire were local, they weren't anyone we knew, really. Not well."

Murray held up a hand. "We didn't even know if they were local at first. People from counties all around here went out to that lake. Still do. It wasn't until Claire Quindlen was killed that we thought the guys were local, and that the murders were connected to her, uh…activities. But that door being unlocked doesn't mean it was somebody she knew well. It could have just been somebody she wasn't afraid of. Could have been the kid who carried her groceries, or your mailman, or your second-grade teacher."

"That's true," Jennifer said. It was something she hadn't really thought of; she'd been so shocked to think her mother had known her killer that she'd assumed she'd known him well. It was still a possibility, but Murray's theory was a comforting one.

"I read the file—we both did—," Daniel said. "We saw the people who were interviewed, mainly the volunteers and the few people who were downtown. But did you ever have any suspicions or theories about anyone she knew?"

"We had heard the rumors that maybe one of the white folks that helped out was actually working for the other side, as it were," Murray answered. "And we talked to all those people but, while they might have told someone else that she was going to be there, all of their alibis checked out, and nobody stood out to us."

Jennifer looked over at Daniel, who was looking at her. She didn't know anything else to ask.

"I see that colored girl from time to time," Murray said. "Your friend that was hurt out at the lake." Jennifer looked back at him. He had that smile again, the one that was almost a smirk. "She's a stunner. I saw her in Pantry Pride not long ago with a wedding ring and a couple of tots. I guess she went with a colored guy after all."

Jennifer felt something cold in her belly. She opened her mouth, but Daniel's voice came out.

"A decorated soldier," he said stonily. "Missing in action."

He stood up, and Jennifer grabbed her purse from the floor and did the same. Murray just smiled, as he pushed himself from the counter and started for the door.

They followed him, with the air between them cooler than it had been, and Roger Miller sounding way too carefree on the stereo. Murray opened the door.

"I can't say I blame you for looking into it, but that trail is stone cold by now," he said. "I'm surprised Ray's even letting you try."

"He's not," Daniel answered as they stepped out. "The case is closed. We just wanted to talk to you. For ourselves."

Murray nodded and smiled, then shut the door behind them.

A few minutes later, they pulled back onto Citrus Trail and turned left toward town.

"I actually dislike him less than I thought I would," Jennifer said.

Daniel looked over at her. "Really. I find that surprising."

She shrugged. "He's smoother than I expected a farting redneck to be."

Ten minutes later, they pulled into a paved driveway and parked next to an older Impala. An even older black Ford pickup was parked on the other side of it. A porch had been built onto the front of the neat trailer home, and Frank Hamilton was sitting on it, not rocking his rocking chair.

Daniel and Jennifer got out of the truck and walked to the porch. Daniel put one foot up on the bottom step.

"Hello, Frank."

Hamilton nodded. "Daniel. Miss Sheehan." His tone was cool, his look stern. His reddish hair had lightened a bit, but was still there, still neatly trimmed and parted on the side. He stood, and Jennifer saw that he was about the same height as Murray, but much trimmer. He wore pressed trousers and shirtsleeves.

"Kenneth told me to expect you," Hamilton said. "I'm not a police officer anymore, and I've put that case behind me, so I'd appreciate it if we could just talk out here."

Daniel nodded. "That's fine."

"I doubt I have anything to add to what he told you. You think someone Claire Quindlen knew killed her. I don't know who that would have been."

Jennifer glanced around her. The lawn was manicured, and multicolored impatiens filled the flower beds on either side of the porch.

"We just thought maybe you'd remember something Murray didn't," Daniel said. "Or remember wondering about somebody without actually having any concrete reason to wonder."

"No." Hamilton looked at Jennifer. "That was a bad time. For all of us. You, especially, I realize. But I doubt there's any profit in digging at all up now. Kenneth and I did our best, I can assure you of that."

"It's not really our intention to dig anything up," Jennifer said, though she wasn't sure that was exactly true. "I'm just trying to put it behind me, too, and

I wanted to see the case files. I saw the door lock, and…" She shook her head.

"We talked to people who knew your mother, your family. We talked to them, too," he said. "Even your father. But none of them became suspects in any way."

"Not even as a gut feeling?" Daniel asked.

He looked down at Daniel. "I act on evidence, not gut feelings, Daniel. You know that. Gut feelings are more Kenneth's area, and I don't remember him having any."

"He's a warm guy," Jennifer said a few minutes later. It startled Daniel, who had been mulling over locked doors and retired cops and cold trails.

He pulled back onto Main Street, which would eventually turn into Citrus Trail. "He was never one of the fun guys. He was a decent cop, though. He drinks. So does Murray, but Murray hangs out at Monty's and drinks with his pals. From what I understand, Hamilton's wife left him back…I don't know, around 1960, something like that. He never remarried, and he drinks alone."

"You know, I'm starting to think that any cop who stays with it a long time becomes a drinker," Jennifer said. "A lot of the guys in New Orleans did. The few women cops I knew didn't; they had husbands and sometimes kids to get home to."

"It does seem to be an occupational danger," Daniel said quietly.

Aside from a few beers here and there, Daniel didn't drink. He'd seen too many guys in Vietnam who found their only peace in a glass, and it had scared him.

He looked over at Jennifer. For the hundredth time, it struck him how much she looked the same, and how much she didn't. She'd filled out a little more, and she had a few tiny little lines starting up around her eyes, but it was more the set of her jaw, and the strength and stubbornness in her eyes. Not for the first time, he realized that she was prettier than she had been before. He tried not to let that distract him.

"What was it like out there?" he asked her. "In New Orleans?"

She looked over at him. "Very different. People there take pride in being outside the mainstream, in being different. Things between blacks and whites weren't as black and white as they were here, no pun intended. It's a beautiful city. You would like it, I think."

Daniel nodded, and stared out at a red light. It finally turned green, and they moved through the intersection where Main Street turned into Citrus Trail.

"I almost went out there, you know," he said quietly.

He saw her head jerk around, but he didn't look at her.

"When?"

He swallowed. "I went to see Grandma the day I enlisted. She told me where you were. I think she wanted me to go out there."

He glanced over at Jennifer, but she was staring out her window.

"I wish you had," she said, almost too quiet for him to catch it. Then she did look at him. "But I don't blame you for not coming. It had been, what, five years?"

"Four."

He looked back out at the road. Just ahead, two black teenaged girls were sitting in aluminum chairs beside the Orange Blossom fruit stand. He remembered the time the four of them had snuck into the grove. It was their junior year. He and Jen had just declared themselves engaged, though he hadn't given her the ring yet, and everything was new and exciting and good.

It had been late on a January Saturday night. They'd been coming back from the movies, and Inez and Jonah made him pull over. They parked behind the fruit stand and ran into the groves, trying not to laugh so loudly the night watchman would catch them. Then they'd climbed a couple of orange trees, Jonah and Inez in one, Daniel and Jen in another one across the way.

They'd sat up in the branches, picking oranges and eating them right there, shivering in the cold. Jen had sat between his legs, leaning back into his chest as he wrapped the sides of his windbreaker around her and she fed him sections one at a time. The oranges had been incredibly sweet and juicy that year, and his life had been simple and good and full of every possibility. All of them had included her, had centered around all four of them always being together. He had had no reason to think it would be otherwise.

He realized the cab of the truck had been quiet just long enough to be uncomfortable. Jen was looking out her window again, nibbling at a thumbnail. He had forgotten that she did that when she was worried or nervous. He wondered which one she was now.

"I was worried that it would go badly," he said. "And then I would go to Vietnam. That it would be bad for me to go there after a bad goodbye. Or that it would go well and then I'd have to leave."

He saw her turn to look at him.

"I wish you had come."

They were quiet again for a few moments, and he supposed they were both thinking about what might have happened. But that was then.

"I almost came home a couple of times," Jennifer said. "Twice I even packed my stuff. Once about a month after I left, and then again right after I graduated high school."

"I was in Fort Lauderdale, looking for you," he said, with a bit more tightness than he'd intended. That trip had been a horrible failure in many ways. He hadn't found his fiancé. He'd spent a lot of time getting drunk at some place called The Elbo Room on the beach, where a lot of people his age hung out. He'd lost his virginity to some girl he couldn't even picture in his head the next day. He badly wanted to ask her when she'd lost hers and with whom, but he damn well wasn't going to.

"So why did you come home?" he asked her.

It took her a minute to answer him, her face still turned to the window.

"I was so tired of being the only person who knew me," she said quietly.

CHAPTER 15

When Jennifer walked into the station the following morning, Messer was already there.

"Hey, Anthony." She put her purse down on her desk.

"Hey," he answered, looking a little nervous. "Ray wants to see you five minutes ago."

"Ray wants us," Daniel said quietly, appearing next to her without warning. "He's somewhat pissed."

Jennifer's chest tightened. "That was fast."

"What'd you guys do?" Anthony asked under his breath.

"Daniel, I'm sorry."

"Why? It was my idea."

"You wouldn't have if I hadn't—" she glanced around the room.

"But you did, and so I would have eventually," Daniel replied in what was almost a stage whisper, almost a hiss. "So, eventually we would have ended up exactly where we are."

"Where the hell are you guys?" Anthony asked. "What did you do?"

Daniel looked at him. "Nothing really wrong."

"We disobeyed Ray's orders."

"And did what, exactly?"

"Maybe you could explain it to him in the car later, when we're not standing in the middle of your ten biggest fans," Daniel said.

Jennifer quickly looked around the room. Half the guys were looking without trying to hide it. The other half were trying.

"Let's get it over with," Jennifer said.

Daniel stepped back and let her pass. She felt all eyes on them as they crossed the room to Ray's open door. He looked up as she was about to knock on the jamb.

"Get in here," he said quietly. "And shut that door."

They stepped in, and Daniel closed the door behind them. Ray watched them walk to the desk. Jennifer sat, Daniel didn't.

Ray put his pen down and sat forward. "Both Frank Hamilton *and* Kenneth Murray called me last night. At home, on a Sunday."

Jennifer swallowed. "They complained?"

"I wouldn't say that, although neither one of them was especially tickled," Ray answered. "Murray was at least kind of curious about your door lock. Hamilton is a sad, sorry man who just wants to be left alone with his garden and his whisky."

"I'm the one who called Murray and asked to come out," Daniel said.

"I don't actually care," Ray said. He looked from him to Jennifer. "I expressly told you that this is *not* an open case, that we did *not* have permission to look into it at this time, and that you were *not* to go poking around."

"I know. I'm sorry, Ray," she said without flinching. "I just really needed to know if one of them unlocked that door."

"And they didn't. So how did that help you, precisely?"

"If they had, she could stop worrying so much about who did," Daniel said.

Ray looked back at him. "But they didn't, so she can't. And I've got two police officers who don't appreciate being reminded, by the very young, inexperienced cop who just happens to be the daughter and sister of two of the victims, that they weren't able to solve the biggest, most divisive case of their careers!"

He rubbed at his face, his mustache stretching with his skin. "And I assure you that half those guys out there know that, and the other half will hear about it the next time they go to Monty's, which isn't gonna help you fit in any better than you already do."

"I wasn't trying to make anything harder than it already is, Ray."

"Don't call me Ray this morning," he said, his voice clipped. "This morning you call me Chief."

"Okay."

"Chief—," Daniel started.

"Be quiet, Daniel. I'm surprised you had anything to do with this."

"With all due respect—,"

"Little late for that, son."

"Jen has a valid point," Daniel said, raising his voice slightly. "The lock matters. And I don't know why you're so surprised. Jonah was my best friend. Jen—these guys didn't just kill her family—"

Ray stood up. "You gonna remind me what was lost? I carried *my* best friend's casket, son. Carried Jonah's, too. Right alongside you, as I recall. Jonah was like a nephew to me."

Ray sat back down and took a breath. "I know what you lost, Daniel," he said, glancing at Jennifer. "But the fact remains that you are both officers with Dismal PD, and you cannot run around opening old wounds and raising new questions without official sanction, and even if we were opening the case again, the two of *you* certainly wouldn't be handling it."

"We know that," Jennifer said. "And when I first asked you for that file, it wasn't about reopening the case or anything like that. I just wanted to know. I wanted to see the facts, as an adult."

"And now you've seen them," Ray said. "And maybe—*maybe*—you noticed something that slipped by everybody back then. It's not enough to look into it officially, and if you look into it even unofficially, you're gonna cause us and a lot of other people a lot of heartache and trouble. Those murders tore this town apart for months. *Months*. If you're gonna pick at scabs, you have to have a better reason than an unlocked door, and I *told* you that the other day."

"Yes, you did," Jennifer said. She was going to be respectful; Ray deserved that. But she wasn't a scared little teenager anymore, and she wasn't going to cringe or whimper.

"Y'all go get ready for muster," Ray said quietly. "And understand something. I love you, Jennifer. And you know how I feel about you, Daniel. But make no mistake. You directly disobey me like that again and I will fire both y'all's asses without hesitation. I cannot keep my people effective *or* safe if they know they can be blatantly insubordinate without consequence."

He looked at Daniel, then at Jennifer. "Y'all understand that well enough this time?"

"I don't know, Jennifer," Anthony was saying. "You got some *cajones*. If it was my brother, my mother, God rest her, I don't know if I could look at those pictures."

"I already saw it all, Anthony," Jennifer replied.

"Still."

He was actually letting her drive, since he was starving and couldn't eat his tuna sandwich and drive at the same time. Jen had already eaten hers. Touchingly, after they'd met, Michelle had started packing lunch for both of them.

"I'll just say this," Anthony said, wiping his mouth with a paper napkin. "I think you've got a right to understand what happened. And if, God forbid it, somebody close to your mom or your family actually did this thing, then you need to know it. Not because they might hurt you, 'cause I think whatever hair got across their butts back then, they're probably over it by now, and it's not like they can get back at her now, right?"

He unwrapped a homemade brownie and took a bite. "But you can't be spending the rest of your life wondering if the guy you sit next to at church, or your family doctor—or whoever— if they killed your family. Right?"

"Right," Jennifer agreed distractedly, and stopped for a red light.

Across the street just past the intersection, there was a cluster of people on the sidewalk out in front of Patterson's. Patterson's was a neighborhood bar that was popular with blue collar workers on the west side of town. The group looked agitated.

"What's going on over here now, while I'm trying to enjoy my brownie?" Anthony asked.

"I don't know."

The light turned green, and Jennifer drove slowly past. Yes, there was something going on. Two men, one young and one in his forties or so, were yelling at each other. There were a few older men standing behind the older man, who wore an electric company uniform, and a matching group of younger men behind the other guy.

"Aw, come on, man," Anthony said. "It's been a nice quiet day so far."

He picked up the radio and called in, as Jennifer made a U-turn and pulled slowly up to the curb. There were no weapons that Jennifer could see, and it didn't look like any punches had been thrown yet, but things were definitely heated. The older guy was facing them, but he barely glanced in their direction before going back to jabbing his finger in the air between himself and the younger guy, who was wearing blue coveralls.

"Alrighty, let's see what's bugging these guys," Anthony said, and they both got out of the car.

Once outside, they could hear a bit better.

"I don't care what you and your fag liberal buddies say!" the older man was saying. "And if you don't like *my* opinions, then you can go find another place to get your beer."

"Maybe you should keep opinions like that to yourself, or tell them to yourself when you're home alone, instead of out here around decent human beings," the younger man yelled. As she got closer, Jennifer thought maybe she knew him.

"What's going on?" Anthony asked mildly as he stepped up behind the group. The younger guys moved back a bit.

The younger man, slightly built, with almost yellow blond hair, jerked his head around. He seemed surprised, but not scared, to see the police. "This guy's ruining my damn lunch running his mouth!"

Jennifer stepped up onto the sidewalk near the older man, who turned to look at her. He did a dramatic double-take and smirked. "Oh, look who it is! Dismal's very own Gloria Steinem." He looked back at his buddies. "That's ironic, huh?"

"Why's that?" Jennifer asked.

"Because he was just talking about your mother," the young man said.

"My mother?" Jennifer looked back at the older guy. "What about her?"

"He's saying she brought it on herself, brought it on the whole town, running around with n— hanging around with black people." He shrugged. "Your mother was a good person."

Jennifer looked at the older guy, who wasn't embarrassed. She looked back at the younger guy, who looked to be about her age. "Do I know you?"

He shrugged. "Probably not. I'm Jason Broderick. I was a couple years behind you in school. But my older sister Patty used to run the cash register for your mom, at her shop."

Jennifer didn't remember, but she nodded like she did.

"Your sister like colored guys, too, there, Jason?" the older guy asked, sneering.

"She's married to a white guy, but so what if she did, you redneck piece of—"

The older guy moved like he was going to get in the Jason kid's face. Jennifer stepped forward and put an arm in front of him, and he slapped it away.

"Hey!" Anthony yelled angrily. He moved toward the older guy, but Jennifer held her right hand up to stop him. Then she pointed at the older guy with her left.

"You put your hands on an officer of the law, and it's felony assault," she said quietly. "You put your hands on *me*, and I'll beat the crap out of you in front of all your friends."

"Is that right?" the older guy asked.

"That's right. And since you made the first move, I'll be watching *Mannix* at home tonight, while you're whining for some Bufferin in jail."

"I'd love to watch that, but I'm gonna be late clocking back in as it is," Jason said. "Can I go?"

"You can go," Anthony answered. Jason and the other younger men headed for the parking lot behind them. Anthony looked at the older guy, whose friends were already heading for Patterson's door. "You going with them or with us?"

"What if I want to press charges or something?"

Jennifer shook her head. As she did, she saw someone standing on the corner across the street.

"For what? Not liking you?" Anthony asked. "I don't think that's illegal. Or uncommon, either."

It was Reggie Goode, or Good Reggie Goode, as people used to call him. He was just standing there, both hands on his cane, smiling at her. He wore gray trousers with sharp creases, a white, short-sleeved shirt with a red bowtie, and a straw bowler.

"I'll be right back," Jennifer said as she stepped off the sidewalk.

As she crossed the street, she saw that his light skin was still unlined, though he had to be at least forty by now. She couldn't see much of his short, curly hair, but what she saw was still black as night.

Reggie Goode had been sent to prison at the age of sixteen, for accidentally killing another boy in a fight. He'd hit the boy, and the boy had struck his head on the edge of a piece of broken concrete. Jennifer couldn't remember what the fight had been about.

Reggie had become a little famous while still a prisoner, when the Chicago Tribune published one of his poems. A bigtime New York publisher published a slim volume of Reggie's poems, and he was the darling of Civil Rights activists for a few months before the press moved on to someone else.

When Reggie had been released at the age of twenty-four, he'd come back home to live with his aging mother. When she passed shortly after, he stayed on, and frequently volunteered with Claire, writing up heartfelt fundraising letters or penning poems that sometimes made the Florida or Alabama papers. Jennifer's mother had adored Reggie. Jonah had once wondered aloud if Reggie were actually a little in love with Claire.

Reggie was in an interesting position in Dismal. He was black, and vocal about Civil Rights and other hot social topics, but the rednecks left him alone. There were rumors that Reggie had killed an older, white man in prison when he was eighteen or nineteen. That he'd not only stabbed the man with the man's own homemade knife, but also cut out his tongue and thrown it away.

The rumors also said he'd killed the man for making advances. Nothing had ever been proven, no one in jail admitted to knowing anything, and Reggie had never been charged. He'd also been smart enough not to deny the rumors once he got home.

His smile got wider as Jennifer stepped up onto the sidewalk. His teeth were still brilliantly white and perfectly straight.

"Well, if it isn't Miss Jenny, come home to little Dismal after all," he said. His voice was gentle and smooth and almost aristocratic. As a kid, she'd loved the way he spoke.

"How are you, Reggie?"

"I'm quite fine, thank you," he answered. "And how are you, my fair one?"

"I'm good, thank you," she replied with a smile. "It's good to see you."

"And it's good to see you as well, though I question the wisdom of your return."

"I wanted to come home. This is my home."

"It used to be, yes," he replied. "But what is here for you to return to? Even your wonderful grandmother is gone."

Jennifer swallowed. "Friends. The house I grew up in."

"Yet your coming is already causing strife," Reggie said, still smiling.

"That? That's not my fault."

"You come home to stir that pot that has been idling on a low flame, and all of the aromas, good and bad, start wafting through the air."

"What do you mean?"

"You are, at the very least, an unpleasant reminder, my Jenny." His smile dimmed a bit, his warm, brown eyes lost the laughter that shone in them. "For the white man, you're a reminder of ugliness and shame. For the black man, loss and injustice."

Jennifer tried to smile, but mostly failed. "Thanks. It's so good to be home."

"Don't misunderstand me. Your home is your birthright, and many of us are happy that you've come back to claim it. Inez, certainly. Young Daniel most assuredly."

Jennifer wasn't in the mood to enlighten him about that one.

"But you're not just here to get back to the soil in which you were cultivated, are you, Jenny?" he asked. "You've come looking for reparation, have you not?"

"If you mean answers, sure," she said.

He smiled at her again, then leaned in and gave her a gentle kiss on the cheek. He smelled of Afro Sheen and Aramis. When he straightened, he tipped his bowler to her with one long, manicured finger. Then he started walking away, his cane tapping gently beside him.

"In the fullness of time, my Jenny," he said over his shoulder. "All truth is revealed in the fullness of time."

CHAPTER 16

It was Mama Tyne's orchestration.

The day after the incident in front of Patterson's, Jennifer went over to the Tynes' to visit with them for a while and immerse herself in their contented noise, rather than going home to the silence of her own house.

Jennifer and Inez were in the bathroom bathing Isaac and Ruthie when Mama Tyne popped into the doorway.

"Jenny. My baby. You need to get Inez out this house," she'd said.

"Oh, come on, Mama," Inez laughed.

"When?" Jennifer had asked the woman.

"This evening, baby," Mama had answered. "This girl's not been out of the house without those kids in months."

"Now, Mama, you know that's not true," Inez said.

"Grocery shopping don't count, little girl." Mama Tyne looked at Jennifer. "After you get these babies bathed, I'll get them into bed. Y'all go do something."

"Okay," Jennifer said.

"Like what?" Inez asked. "I don't feel like making myself presentable just so I can say I left the house."

"Why don't you just come over to the house, then?" Jennifer asked her. "We can watch a movie or something?"

"Y'all don't have to get all *that* wild," Mama Tyne said.

"I'm tired, mama. Besides, Jen and I like just hanging out."

"We could make some caramel corn," Jennifer said, smiling.

"See, Mama? We'll get good and wild."

Forty-five minutes later, they pulled into Jennifer's driveway, and she groaned. Daniel's truck was parked there.

"So what?" Inez asked, laughing. "Daniel can eat caramel corn, too."

"I just—"

"You just what? You don't want me watching you two watch each other?"

"No. We don't do that," Jennifer said. "I just don't know how to be when we're around each other."

"Be? Who else are you gonna be? Shut up and get out of the car."

Daniel was sitting on the top porch step, toothpick in his mouth, wearing jeans and an Alabama jersey.

"Hey," he said.

"Hey, Daniel," answered Inez.

"Hey. What's up?" Jennifer asked.

"What do you mean, what's up?" He stood up.

Jennifer shrugged. "You just come by to say hello or what?"

Daniel squinted first at her, and then at Inez. "No, I did not," he told Jennifer snippily. "Mama Tyne said you guys wanted me to come over and watch a movie."

Inez laughed. "Daniel. You're a cop. Did you ask her why *she* was telling you that?"

He looked at her, one side of his mouth curving upward. "Well, no, as a matter of fact."

Jennifer felt her face go warm.

"So, what is she up to?" Daniel asked.

Inez waved him off. "Ah, she just wants us all together again. All her little babies." She looked at Jennifer. "So, are we gonna watch a movie or what?"

"Yeah. Come on," Jennifer said, walking to the door.

"So, do you actually want me to stay, or should I go hang out with Mama Tyne?"

"Yes, we want you to stay," Jennifer said. "Geez."

She unlocked and opened the door. She always left the lamp on by the front door, but she went ahead and turned on the overhead light as well, and led them inside.

"You got a TV Guide around here?" Inez asked.

"On the coffee table," Jen answered. "You guys take your shoes off, get comfortable. I'm gonna go put my things away and change into some shorts or something."

Jennifer heard Inez telling Daniel about caramel corn as she walked down the dark hallway to her bedroom. She reached in and flipped the light switch, and felt her world tilt just a little.

"Daniel!" she shouted without meaning to.

She heard him hurrying to the hallway, and then she heard Inez right behind him.

"What's wrong?" Inez called.

Jennifer swung around as she heard Daniel stop behind her. "Don't let her in here!" she yelled.

Daniel's eyes widened as he took in the room for just a second.

"What's wrong, Jen?" Inez called, her tone now touched with alarm.

Daniel spun around and grabbed Inez by the shoulders. "Go—just go back out there for a minute."

"Inez, go back to the living room!" Jennifer said.

"Why? No. What's wrong?"

"Inez, just go!"

"Inez, honey, just go wait for us—" Daniel said.

Inez pushed past him, flinging his hand from her shoulder. "Get off me, Daniel! What's go—"

She looked first at Jennifer, like she was checking her for injury, but then she looked past Jennifer. She stopped dead, and her mouth hung open just a bit. Her eyes grew immediately, impossibly, wide as she looked at the wall in front of her.

"Don't look at them, Inez," Jennifer said.

"What is this?" Inez asked quietly.

She slowly turned around where she stood, her eyes flicking from one wall to another. All of them covered with 8x10, black and white pictures. Daniel came into the room beside her, and they all looked around in silence.

Every wall was covered with the pictures of dead people that they had loved.

Jennifer looked over at Inez, and she felt helpless as she watched tears slide down her beautiful friend's beautiful face, as she watched her walk slowly over to the wall where Jennifer's dresser was.

Just at Inez's eye level was a picture of Jonah lying on a sheet on the ground. His head had turned toward the camera, and his eyes were open, looking at nothing, looking surprised. A hank of his blond hair had fallen across his forehead, and there was a smear of blood in it.

Inez reached out slowly, her hand trembling, and touched the photograph.

"Inez, let's go out of the room," Daniel said.

She turned around, looked first at him, then at Jennifer. "What the hell is happening?" she asked softly. "Why are these here?"

Jennifer swallowed hard. "I don't know."

"Where'd they come from?"

Jennifer glanced over at Daniel, then back at Inez. "They were in the kitchen."

"Were the doors locked when you left?" Daniel asked her.

"Yeah, but they're just flimsy old locks."

"You telling me somebody came in here, come in Grammy's house, and put these up on your wall?" Inez asked, incredulous. Her reddish-brown curls bobbed, and there was a shiny line from her nose to her upper lip.

Jennifer looked at Daniel.

"Why do you even have these things?" Inez asked her, bending at the waist to make Jennifer look at her.

"I got them from Ray."

Inez looked from one to the other. "Y'all aren't seeing each other; you're looking for them, aren't you?" She looked at Daniel. "Aren't you?"

"Not really," answered Jennifer. "I just—we wanted to look at the file."

Inez pointed over her shoulder at the wall behind her. "And who was in your house? In your *bedroom*? Putting pictures of *our* people all over your walls?"

"I don't know."

"You don't know," she said softly.

"I'm getting these down," Daniel said. "Do you have any gloves?"

"Just Grandma's dishwashing gloves."

He nodded, then walked out of the room. Jennifer looked at Inez. Tall, stunning Inez, who looked like a frail flower suddenly, as she stared at another picture of Jonah.

"Inez..." Jennifer started.

Inez looked at her, her face stricken, then suddenly covered her mouth and ran out of the room.

Jennifer sat on the side of the old tub, holding a yellow-flowered hand towel in her lap. Inez spat a mouthful of water into the sink, then cupped her hand under the faucet to get another. She swished it around in her mouth before spitting it out, too, then splashed a couple of handfuls of water over her face. The light reflected in a rivulet that ran from her delicate chin.

She turned off the water and looked at Jennifer, and Jennifer handed her the hand towel. Inez took it and held it to her face for a moment, then sat down on the side of the tub next to Jennifer, their shoulders touching.

"I'm sorry," Jennifer said softly. Inez nodded. "What can I do?"

"You can shoot 'em in their face," Inez answered quietly. "Just shoot 'em, 'cause people like that have no right to live in this world."

Jennifer swallowed. She had no response to that. Inez looked over at her.

"That person was in this *house*," she said. "In your *room*, where you sleep and stand around naked and don't look for evil people to be under your bed. Do you understand what I'm saying?"

"Yes." Jennifer took the hand towel from Inez, just for something to do, somewhere else to look. She stood up and arranged it on the pink porcelain towel bar.

"I need a drink," Inez said behind her. Jennifer turned around. "Tell me Grammy made some of her blackberry wine before she died."

Jennifer pulled a full quart jar down from a shelf in one of the kitchen cupboards, then turned and showed it to Inez, who sat at the table.

"Blackberry wine?" Inez asked.

"Elderberry tincture," Jen answered. "There's no wine."

"Oh, that stuff tasted so awful," Inez said. "What's in it?"

"Vodka."

"Gimme some."

Jennifer reached into another cupboard and got two small glasses down. She poured them each an inch or two, then handed Inez a glass as Daniel walked into the kitchen with the accordion file.

"I'll give these to Ray in the morning," he said, putting the file on the counter.

"Oh, this is foul!" Inez exclaimed.

Jennifer had just taken a mouthful, and she winced as she swallowed.

"What is that?" Daniel asked.

"Elderberry tincture," Inez answered.

He put his hands on his hips. "Y'all have colds, now?"

Jennifer coughed. Inez held out her empty glass. Daniel took it and held it out to Jennifer, who poured another couple of glugs into it. Daniel took a swallow, then coughed as he handed it to Inez.

"Oh, man," he said roughly. "Is that grain alcohol?"

"Vodka," Jennifer said.

"I'll take some."

Jennifer got another glass and poured some tincture into it, then handed it to him. He pulled a .38 from the back waistband of his jeans and set it on the counter.

"You just carry that around now, like you're on *Streets of San Francisco*?" Inez asked.

"No, wiseass. I got it out of the truck while you were in the bathroom." He took a swallow of the tincture, then winced as it went down. "Whoo. That's hard."

He shook his head and took another sip, then looked at Jennifer. "The lock on the utility room door is all scratched up, and it was unlocked when I checked it. Did you open it before you went to Inez's house?"

"No." Jennifer shook her head. "I never use it. I just use this door," she said, pointing behind her at the back door.

"Well, I'm sure there are all kinds of prints all over it, but we can see if Ray will send somebody out to dust the knob and the door."

Jennifer shook her head. “It’ll still be there tomorrow morning. I really want to try to keep this as quiet as we can. Ray’s gonna flip to begin with, and for all we know, the person that did this isn’t even one of the guys that killed Mom and the boys.”

“But it probably is.”

“Probably. But it could have just been someone who broke in here to ransack the house or cut up my underwear, whatever, just to scare me, and they saw those pictures and got a better idea.”

“This is crazy,” Inez said. “I can’t believe we have to talk about stuff like this. Again. Still.”

“I know,” Jennifer said. “I’m sorry.”

Inez looked at the two of them, then looked around the kitchen slowly. “Man, I love this house. I always loved this house. We had some good times here, y’all.”

Jennifer nodded. “We’ll have more.”

“Yeah.” Inez finished her glass, and held out her other hand, wiggling her fingers. Jennifer handed her the jar. “Hey, you remember the time you polished your doll baby black?”

The two women smiled. Daniel looked at Inez. “I don’t know this story.”

“Yeah, you do,” Inez said, waving him off.

“We were like six or seven,” Jennifer said. “I think it was only the second or third time Inez had been over. Anyway, when she had been over before, I had felt badly when we were playing dolls, because all my dolls were white."

"So, the next time I come over here with Mama, we go in the room, and this girl's gone and painted one of her dolls black with Grammy's shoe polish. Mama never did get it all out of my dress."

Jennifer smiled and looked over at Daniel. He was smiling at the floor, but it looked like a sad smile, somehow.

"Come on, y'all," Inez said, standing and stretching. "We aren't gonna sit here in this kitchen and talk about what was going on in your bedroom, or nothin' like that. Let's go see what's on TV."

They didn't find anything in the TV Guide that they felt like watching.

Jennifer felt an uncomfortable awkwardness between them, trying to hang out in her living room like they had done on so many nights, so many nights ago. That slowly dissipated, and their attempts at cheerfulness became less forced, with each little glass of Grandma's elderberry cough syrup. They weren't drunk by the time someone turned on the radio, but they had a good buzz on, owing to the fact that none of them actually drank hard liquor.

It started with Inez finding "Touch Me in the Morning" on the radio. She whirled around to face them, a slender arm flowing high through the air, as she belted it out along with Diana Ross. Jennifer had forgotten how well she sang.

And then they were dancing in the middle of the living room, with the lamps all unplugged and set aside on one of the chairs, and Grandma's rag rug rolled up and leaning against a wall. They danced to "Shambala," their arms in the air, all of them singing along with "Three Dog Night."

They had always loved dancing together. Jennifer had always loved to watch Inez, and had learned to dance from her, though never as well. Daniel was an excellent dancer, and she had loved to dance with him, had loved to watch him, too.

And now they all danced together, with their little glasses of medicine in their hands, and pretended that they hadn't spent the last eleven years apart, and that none of them felt the empty space where Jonah would have been. They danced like it was a spell they were casting to ward off the evil that had been in Jennifer's room.

They did the bump to "Rock the Boat", with Inez in the middle, and Jennifer took a break on the couch and watched Daniel twirl Inez around to "Will It Go 'Round in Circles." She smiled as she watched them, the two most important people she had left in her life. They were, at once, both eighteen and almost-thirty, and they were beautiful to her.

She glanced toward the kitchen, and saw Grandma in the doorway, swinging her hips and waving her hands by her ears. She thought about asking Daniel and Inez if they could see Grandma, too, but then she was gone.

When "If You Could Read My Mind" came on, Inez shamed Jennifer and Daniel into slow dancing while she made some snacks. It was as though the two of them had been intentionally crafted to fit each other so well, and Jennifer was instantly overwhelmed by both memory and the present. By the way his chest was warm against hers, and how she could feel his breath on her neck as his temple rested against hers. He used a different shampoo now, and it smelled of apples. His hand was warm and slightly damp, more calloused than it had been the last time they'd danced.

Neither of them said anything at all, through the entire song. He was too close for talk to seem natural to Jennifer. She didn't know why he was quiet, or what his thoughts were. So, Gordon Lightfoot did all the talking, and when he was done, Jennifer was glad to see Inez return from the kitchen with a bowl of Fritos in her hand.

Jennifer and Daniel sat on the couch later, their feet on the coffee table, with an empty space between them where Inez had been. Inez was swaying in front of the stereo, finding a station that wasn't playing Helen Reddy. She stopped on "Rock Your Baby," then turned around and took a sip from her glass. She looked at them, and a slow smile spread across her face.

"Y'all are so beautiful," she said. "But I'm still mad at you. I got to pee."

She disappeared down the hall, and Daniel and Jennifer sat in silence for a moment.

"She thought we were seeing each other again," Daniel said finally, not looking at her.

"Yeah."

After a moment, he looked over at her. "Are you seeing anybody?"

Jennifer's chest constricted, and her ears warmed. Did it matter to him? Did it matter to her?

"No," she answered. He nodded. "Although, I might be in love with Jim Stafford. Does that count?"

"Are you sleeping with him?"

"No."

"Then no."

Inez walked back into the room. "I gotta get Ruthie some of that pink toilet paper; she'd love that."

Daniel didn't want Inez to go out on the back porch alone, so when she went out for a cigarette, he followed.

He declined her offer of a cigarette, but took her Zippo from her and lit hers. She blew smoke off to the side, then took her lighter back and shoved it into the back pocket of her cut-offs.

There was a nice breeze, cool for July, and it felt good on his face and neck. He looked out at the back yard, full of shadows and loud with frogs and crickets.

"You're gonna stay here tonight," Inez said quietly.

"Yeah, I'm staying," he said. "Are you staying, too?"

"No, I gotta make sure I'm there when Mama leaves for work at six," she answered.

"I'll take you home."

"No, you won't," Inez said. "You're still buzzed. I'll call Rudy or Bobby to come bring me home."

He studied her profile as she stared out at the yard. He'd always been fascinated by the fact that she seemed so delicate, and yet was actually so strong. She'd had enough mettle to comfort him while she was still grieving Jonah, and he was embarrassed to remember that. Yet, she'd told him that he had held her together. He didn't understand why they hadn't seen more of each other since she'd been home.

"I probably shouldn't drive anyway," he said to her now.

"No, that wouldn't look too good, you being a cop and everything," she said. She looked at him. "You and Jen both, cops. Blows my mind. And now you think you're detectives, and you're gonna find the people that killed our people. But they know *you*, and they *found* you."

"We're going to do our best, Inez. To find them. That wasn't really the point before, but it is now, and I'll do whatever I have to do."

"You'll take care of our Jenny, that's what you'll do. You understand me, right?"

"Of course, I will." He looked away from her, focused on the old shed. "Even though we're not together, I still care about her."

"Don't jive me, Daniel."

He looked at her. He didn't need to ask her what she meant, and he didn't much want to talk about it, either.

"Look, Inez. I know you think Jen and I should just pick up where we left off, but it doesn't work that way. I don't work that way."

"What are you so afraid of? She's back, and she's the same person you loved so hard, and I *know* how much you loved her, you know I do. She's the same person, only wiser and stronger and not so scared anymore."

"You think what I feel or don't feel is all there is to it," he said, and chewed his lip in frustration. "You think she's gonna stay, Inez? Really? *She* might even think she will, but she'll either find out who killed everybody, or she'll get tired of trying, and she'll turn right around and go back where she came from. She's been living in New Orleans, Inez. You think Dismal's gonna make her happy?"

Inez stood up, took one last drag, then threw her smoke out into the yard. "I think you're working real hard to forget what *did* make her happy." She started for the screen door. "The brownies smell done."

CHAPTER 17

"Fingerprints aren't going to do us much good right off the bat," Ray said. "We can weed out the prints for whoever we have print cards for. Murray and Hamilton, you all, pretty much any cop in the department back then…"

He sat back and sighed. "That's what we can do the fastest, but it'll probably take a couple days. Then we can try matching any other prints, if we have decent ones, with anybody we looked at back then that's got an arrest record and fingerprints on file. Bo Pruitt, that card-carrying KKK freak they thought about. He's been in jail I don't know how many times. Some of his buddies, too."

He looked up at Daniel and Jennifer, who stood in front of his desk. He'd already gotten the reprimands and 'I told you so's' out of the way, and now he just looked tired already, at barely seven in the morning.

"Cooper's pretty good at dusting for prints. If there are any on your door, he's your best shot at getting them. But, sending him out there on the QT doesn't mean much; the whole department will know about this by the end of the day. It's not like half of 'em haven't already talked to Murray down at Monty's by now."

"Is this enough to reopen the case?" Daniel asked. "I mean, clearly somebody's upset about that."

"No, somebody's upset about her being here," Ray said. "Is it more likely that one of our killers did this? I don't know. Why would they bother? Why call attention to themselves, or the case? More likely than not, it's somebody that just wanted to scare Jennifer, maybe because they know the killers, maybe because they still hate the family. It might even be because they don't like having a female cop. You said the file was sitting right out on the kitchen table. They might have just lucked into a cool way to scare the tar out of you, Jen."

"I know," Jennifer said. "I don't know what the point would be, either, for the killers. It seems like trying to scare me like this would be counterproductive."

"These guys aren't like us, though," Daniel said. "These guys are full of hate, and hatred makes you stupid."

Ray rubbed at his face. "Look, regardless of who or why, and we might not know who or why anytime soon, I think you should come stay with us for a little while, Jennifer."

"Ray—" Jennifer started.

He held up a hand. "I can't get any kind of watch authorized for your house based on this. That's pitiful, I know, but we're already stretched too thin as far as payroll. Hell, we're barely *making* payroll as it is. This town isn't exactly loading us up with tax money. The mayor's just gonna tell me that if this person wanted to hurt you, they could have just waited on you to get home. But, it sure as heck isn't a good idea for you to be out there alone, and maybe it's not even a great idea for you to go stay with your friend, Inez."

"I thought the same thing last night: that if they actually wanted to hurt me, they could have done it. I don't want to go anywhere, Ray."

She didn't know how to explain to him that these people had taken everything else from her. *Everything* else. They weren't going to take her home, too. Ray shook his head and was about to reply when Daniel spoke up.

"I was planning to stay out there," he said quietly. "At least for a little bit."

Jennifer and Ray both stared at Daniel. This was news to Jennifer. Daniel looked at her.

"I stayed on the couch last night. I can do it again."

Jennifer's head was filled with all kinds of reasons she liked the idea, and all kinds of reasons she didn't.

"Is that wise?" Ray asked, looking from Daniel to Jennifer. "Y'all? Or are y'all back together already?"

"No," she and Daniel both answered.

"But that doesn't mean we shouldn't try to be friends," Daniel said.

"No, there's no reason you shouldn't be friends, if you can," Ray said. "But there's lots of reasons that people shouldn't think you're shacking up. That'll cost Jennifer her job."

"Why automatically me?" Jennifer asked without thinking.

Ray gave her a look. "Because that's how the real world is, hon."

Daniel looked at Jennifer. "What do you want to do?"

Jennifer shrugged, and tried to look like it was no big deal to have him stay with her. "If you're okay with staying out at the house for a day or two, I'd appreciate that."

Daniel looked at Ray, who threw up a hand. "I can't tell you not to, and if Jen's not gonna come stay with us, then I'd at least want somebody with her."

"Okay." Daniel nodded.

"Do me a favor and give Jen and me a minute," Ray said.

"All right." Daniel looked at each of them, then walked out of the office, shutting the door behind him.

Ray looked at Jennifer and sighed. "You know what you're doing, there?" he asked, nodding after Daniel.

"We're just trying to..." Jennifer shook her head. "It would be good if we could be friends."

"Listen, I'll feel better about you being out there if he's with you. I don't want you to come to any harm." He shook his head. "But there's all kinds of ways to get hurt."

Jennifer intentionally took her time closing out her shift, to give Daniel a good lead on her. He was going home to pack a few things, then meet her out at the house. Jennifer had to stop at Pantry Pride, anyway, so Daniel would definitely beat her there.

She had just locked her lap drawer when Anthony walked up to her. She'd thought he'd left ten minutes earlier.

He put his hands on his hips, and spoke in a low voice. "What's this crap with a break-in at your house?"

Jennifer sighed. "Who told you about it?"

"Ray. He said to be a little extra alert when we're out on patrol."

Jennifer shrugged. "Yeah, somebody broke in."

"Why?"

She shrugged again, and wished she'd stop shrugging. "Because I'm back? Because maybe I've been looking into what happened in '62?"

She looked around the bullpen. No one was close by. Most of day shift was gone, most of night shift was already out. Patterson was still at his desk, though, and looking at her. She curled her lip at him and looked back at Anthony.

"Why didn't you tell me that?" he asked her.

"About the break-in?"

"Well, yeah," he answered sarcastically. "But maybe about the case, too. I'm your partner, Jennifer. I should maybe know that, especially since we're together all day every day. If somebody's coming after you or something, I should've known about it already. Not just for your safety, but mine."

"That's true. You're right. I'm sorry, Anthony."

"Maybe you should come stay with me and Michelle," he said. "Our loveseat's too short even for you, but we can put a pallet down in the baby's room."

Jennifer smiled. "That's really nice, Anthony. I appreciate it. But I've got people staying with me."

He nodded, but looked reluctant. "We gotta be straight with each other, you know? I'm not trying to scold you or anything, but that's what partners gotta do."

Jennifer nodded. "You're right. I promise I will be."

Anthony nodded, and Jennifer stood up and pulled her purse onto her shoulder. "I'm gonna run. I'll see you in the morning, okay?"

"Yeah, okay."

Patterson watched Jennifer cross the room, and Jennifer held his stare until she was past him. He needed another hobby.

CHAPTER 18

Daniel was waiting in his truck when Jennifer got home just before six. He got out as she shut off her car. She was surprised to see that he was still in uniform.

"Hey," he said as she got out.

"Hey. Why are you sitting in the truck? The porch is cooler."

"I just got here," he said.

He pulled an Army duffle out of the passenger side of his truck. She opened her back door and pulled out the bag of groceries she'd picked up.

"You need any help?" he asked.

"No, it's just this," she answered.

She led the way to the front door and unlocked it. They'd closed and locked the windows before they'd left that morning, both of them grateful for something to do besides stand around looking uncomfortable. Awkward about the night before, awkward about waking up in the same house.

Daniel dropped his duffle on the couch as they passed through the living room, then followed her into the kitchen.

It was overcast and gloomy out, and looked more like eight o' clock than six. Jennifer flipped on the kitchen light, then set the groceries down on the counter. She pulled a pack of thin rib-eyes from the bag and set them on the counter.

"I got us some steaks for dinner. Is that okay?" She turned around to look at him. He was standing in the middle of the room, looking odd there, in full uniform.

"Sure. That's fine."

"You're still in uniform," she said, for something to say.

"I wanted to make sure I was already here when you got home," he said, then looked uncomfortable about his phrasing.

She felt it, too. It was her home, not theirs, and they weren't a couple just coming home after work. She swallowed. It did have a hint of intimacy or familiarity to it, intimacy and familiarity that they didn't have.

She wished they were as comfortable as they'd been the night before, with Inez and a few glasses of elderberry tincture between them.

"I'm just going to change out of mine real quick," she said. "Then I'll fix dinner. If you want to take a shower, there are clean towels in the linen closet in the hallway."

"That's okay. I'll wait until after dinner," he said. He did unbuckle his gun belt, though, and laid it over the back of one of the kitchen chairs.

"Well, I'll be right back."

Daniel followed her back into the living room, and stopped by the coffee table. "Did we drink all of that stuff?"

She stopped and turned around. He was holding one of their glasses. "Yeah," she said, smiling.

"Well, we don't need any tonight." He put the glass back down.

"No."

She headed for her bedroom. No, they did not. He wasn't here to have fun. He was here because he felt obligated to watch over her. She was touched, but also regretted that it wasn't anything more than that.

She dumped her purse by the nightstand, then took her weapon from her belt. She was about to put it in the drawer, as she usually did, but set it down on the nightstand instead. Then she grabbed a pair of shorts and a T-shirt from her dresser and started getting undressed.

Daniel looked around the living room. There was a time when Jennifer's Grandma's living room had been as familiar as his own. He and Jen hadn't spent an awful lot of time apart, especially those last several months, after he'd given her the engagement ring. The ring that was at his house now, in a cigar box full of pictures that he didn't look at much, either.

Even though patrolmen didn't make much money, and his budget was frequently tight, he'd bought Susan a different ring when he'd proposed to her. He'd thought about giving her Jen's ring, but only for a moment. It would have been disrespectful to Susan, but it had felt even more disrespectful to Jen. No, not to Jen; to him *and* Jen, to what they had had and planned. Although, by that time, he had not only stopped expecting Jen to come back, he had also stopped wanting her to.

He wasn't saving the ring for her. He wasn't saving it for anything, and probably should take it to Carter's Jewelry and sell it back to them. It had been the kind of ring that a high school senior pulling extra hours could afford: nice, but not impressive.

It wouldn't bring much, but it wasn't doing him any good sitting in the bottom drawer of his dresser.

He saw the TV Guide sitting on the coffee table, and bent to pick it up, just for something to do. He felt awkward and unsure, a stranger but not a stranger. Belonging but not. It was when he bent over the table that he heard it.

He knew that creak intimately. He'd forgotten he knew it until this morning, when he'd gone into Grandma's room to check the windows, and had stepped on the loose plank just inside her door. He had smiled this morning, remembering all the times he and Jen had stopped making out, had hurriedly straightened out their clothes, because they'd heard that creak. He wasn't smiling now.

He hesitated only the barest moment, bent over the table. He glanced over at the door without lifting his head, as he picked up the TV Guide. The door was cracked open. It hadn't been this morning. He distinctly remembered shutting it when he'd walked back out.

He straightened up, and opened the TV Guide, looked down at the listings for two days ago. His weapon was in the kitchen, a good forty feet away, and past Grandma's door. Jen was in her bedroom, changing. Her weapon was with her, or already in her nightstand drawer. Her room was only about ten feet closer than the kitchen, but it was the opposite way.

It was possible the person in that bedroom was unarmed, but not very likely. He couldn't see a reasonably intelligent person lying in wait for a cop in her own house without having a gun.

He was about to call to her about watching some TV, to try to casually walk to her room with the TV Guide in his hand, when he heard her coming down the short hallway. He turned his back to Grandma's door, and looked at Jen as she came back into the room in shorts and a T-shirt.

Daniel was standing there with the open TV Guide in his hands when Jen walked back into the living room. TV would probably be good. They were stuck alone together, and neither one of them seemed to know how to act, what to say, how to be casual friends.

"You want to watch some TV?" she asked. "I think *The Alamo*'s on tonight. Do you still like westerns?"

He had a weird look on his face as she approached him. He dropped the TV Guide back on the table, then reached out and took her hand. It startled her.

"I don't want to watch TV," he said quietly.

"Okay," Jen said, hesitantly.

He gently pulled her toward him. The look in his eyes was intense, urgent. It scared her a little, and yet it didn't. She felt a swirl of thrill in the pit of her stomach.

"Let's go to your room," he said soothingly.

"What?" she asked, in barely a whisper.

He reached up and his hand brushed a bit of hair from the side of her face. Then he dropped her hand and cupped her face in both hands, the way he used to do, a long time ago.

"I want to make love to you," he said.

Jennifer didn't have time to react. Her mouth opened just a little, to ask him what he was doing, when he bent and kissed her. It was a gentle kiss, sweet, and so familiar that she felt her eyes warm, felt tears getting ready to form. She forced them back, and had just started to return his kiss when he lifted his face from hers, his eyes searching hers, for something. Permission? Reaction?

"It'll be just like the first time, all over again," he said intently, and suddenly her chest filled with ice.

He bent his head again, touched his lips to her temples once, twice, then nuzzled her ear.

"Someone's in Grandma's room," he whispered in her ear.

CHAPTER 19

It felt wrong. It felt wrong and unkind, but he didn't know what the hell else he could do. He was relieved to see her eyes widen just a bit, for just an instant. She understood.

"Okay," she said. "If you're sure."

"I'm sure."

He took her hand again and nodded, and she led him to the bedroom. Her heart was still pounding, but for an entirely different reason. Someone was in the house, and they had just turned their backs to him. It was an incredible effort to walk casually to her room, rather than run.

She could hear her blood pounding in her ears as she pulled Daniel into her room. Her eyes went immediately to her weapon sitting on the nightstand, and she looked over her shoulder. Daniel nodded at her.

She stepped quickly, silent in her bare feet, to the nightstand and carefully picked up her weapon. She couldn't hear anything from beyond her door. She turned around to face Daniel, who was still in the middle of the room, watching the door. He looked over at her.

She was grateful now for the double action of the Chief's. The hammer would have been as loud as a gunshot itself in the thick silence that surrounded them. She brought the revolver up to her midriff, her thumb trembling just a bit against the side. From where she was, she was a sitting duck, but could only see about three feet of the hallway wall across from her door. She wasn't sure who would see whom first.

She glanced at the half-open bedroom door, then looked at him as she took a step forward. When she had his eye, she glanced at and nodded slightly toward the door. He looked over his shoulder at her, then back at her. Then he just barely shook his head.

He stepped over to her silently, then reached out and pulled her almost against him, his back placed squarely and openly toward the door. She pulled her weapon from between them and let her hand fall down and slightly behind her right thigh.

She couldn't help it, didn't know where it came from, the tear that suddenly slid onto her cheek.

"You know I love you, Jen," Daniel said, slightly louder than he might have, but not so loudly as to sound unnatural.

"I love you, too," she said, her throat thick. She wrapped her left arm around him, pressed her palm against his back, which was moist and warm.

He had her face in one hand, and he threaded his fingers through her hair again. "It'll be okay. I promise."

Then he bent his head and kissed the left side of her neck, giving her a clear view of her bedroom door from the right. They stood there for minutes, or seconds, Daniel's heart pounding against her shoulder, her eyes glued to what she could see of the hallway.

Daniel rested his face against hers, his breaths warm and slow against her cheek. She could feel his heart pounding against her shoulder.

Her breathing slowed, and it seemed to take half an hour for her next heartbeart, and another half hour still before she saw the shadow.

She pressed her hand into Daniel's back, and felt him tense from the ground up. To her, it seemed like she raised her weapon so slowly, but her gun arm straightened out just as his arm appeared ahead of him in the doorway, gun raised. She waited until his body began to follow his arm, then she shot Frank Hamilton in the chest.

Daniel pushed her away and spun around as Hamilton was falling against the wall opposite her door. Jennifer recovered her footing as Daniel took two running steps toward Hamilton and was on him.

Hamilton had only a loose hold on his weapon, and Daniel brought his arm down on the man's wrist. The gun skittered on the floor between them, and Daniel grabbed Hamilton by the shoulders and pushed him down in Jennifer's doorway. As Hamilton fell, Jennifer saw the blood blossoming just under his right shoulder.

Daniel was on Hamilton's back, pulling his right arm behind him. Jennifer turned just enough to yank her cuffs from the gun belt hanging on her open closet door. She was moving to give them to Daniel when he snarled at Hamilton.

"You should have just stuck with the scary pictures," he said.

Jennifer saw a flash of confusion on Hamilton's face as she reached to hand Daniel her cuffs, and then Hamilton suddenly reared up and drove the back of his head into Daniel's nose.

Daniel's grip loosened, and Hamilton tossed him to the side as Jennifer raised her gun again. But he scrambled back out the doorway before she could get a clear shot, and she saw him sweep up his gun as he ran.

Daniel jumped up, blood pouring from his nose, and put a hand up as he spun around toward the door. “Stay here!” he yelled.

He ran out of the bedroom. Jennifer could hear Hamilton crashing into something in the living room.

She ran after them.

Daniel was several steps behind him when Hamilton cleared the hallway and turned left, headed for the front door. Daniel got to the end of the hallway as he heard the front door crash open, and he headed for the kitchen. He lost three precious seconds as he stopped by the kitchen chair, unsnapped his holster, and freed his weapon.

He heard bare feet pounding from behind him, and looked over his shoulder expecting Jennifer to run into the kitchen. Instead, he saw her back as she ran out the front door. He cursed, lost another two seconds unlocking the back door and jerking the slide lock back. The door slammed against the wall as he ran through it, around the porch, and across the yard.

He could hear Hamilton running through the woods at the side of the house. There was too much undergrowth to go through them quietly.

Out of the corner of his eye he saw Jennifer hit the woods from the driveway, and he pumped his legs harder. As his heart pounded in his throat and his own breath filled his ears, he saw her running down that alley the other day, saw her frown at him as she told him she could still outrun him.

He was about even with her, twenty or so yards to her left. He could hear Hamilton maybe twenty or thirty feet ahead of her. Enough of a head start to stop, turn, and take aim.

Then he heard her cry out, and hit the ground. His first instinct was to help her. His second was that she was safer with a broken ankle.

Jennifer slammed into the ground face first, her free hand underneath her, instinctively trying to break her fall. Her wrist screamed at her, and her shin was on fire from where it had connected with a huge old tree root.

It took a second for her to get her breath. She heard Daniel moving ahead of her, heard his foot-falls in the leaves, and his loud breaths as he crashed through the underbrush.

She pushed herself up, took a couple of cautious steps that told her that her leg wasn't hurt, then broke into a run again.

Hamilton had enough of a lead on Daniel. If it were her, she'd stop just long enough to turn around and wait, then blow him away. The thought made her suddenly nauseous, and she ran harder, her heart feeling like it would pound right out of her chest.

She heard more noise up ahead, new noise. Then she heard a man's voice cry out, though she couldn't tell whose it was or what they said.

Then she heard a shot, followed not one second later by two more shots in quick succession.

"Daniel!" she yelled without knowing she was going to. "Daniel!"

She heard another man's voice, and was still trying to pick it out when she burst through a line of young oaks and into the barest of clearings.

Daniel was standing there, his chest rising and falling, his breaths loud and shallow. Hamilton was lying face down on the ground about ten feet in front of him, his gun still in his outstretched hand. Anthony, still in uniform, was rushing toward him, his gun trained on him. Just a few yards past Hamilton stood Ray, who was just lowering his weapon. Then Patterson came crashing through the trees from the left. He lowered his weapon as he saw Anthony check for Hamilton's pulse.

Jennifer walked toward Daniel as Anthony looked up and shook his head at Ray. Ray slid his weapon back into his arm holster.

Daniel looked over at her, his face gleaming with perspiration in the setting sun. "You okay?"

She still hadn't quite caught her breath. She nodded, then looked at Ray.

"Frank Hamilton," Ray said quietly, looking at the man's body. "I'll just be damned." He shook his head sadly.

Jennifer and Daniel walked over to the other men.

"What are you doing here?" Daniel asked.

"I thought maybe it would be a good idea to see if I could get a couple of off-duty volunteers."

Jennifer looked at Anthony and smiled. He just nodded.

She and Daniel both looked at Patterson, and the blond officer holstered his weapon and then looked up at Jennifer and frowned. "What? I've got a mother, too."

CHAPTER 20

Inez and Jennifer stood side-by-side at the kitchen counter, Inez sautéing onions and garlic, Jennifer rubbing some salt and pepper into the steaks she and Daniel hadn't eaten the other night.

"Hamilton's sister told Ray that his wife left him for a black man," Jennifer said quietly.

"Really?" Inez asked, looking up at her.

"Yeah, about a year before Jonah, Mom and Ned were killed."

Inez shook her head. "Hate comes from all kinds of places," she said. "All kinds of hurts."

"I don't feel sorry for him," Jennifer said firmly.

"Oh, I don't, either," Inez said. "It just never stops surprising me, the reasons that people do things."

Jennifer heard the front screen door open and then slap shut. Daniel coming back from loading his tool kit into his truck. He'd installed deadbolts on all three of her doors.

"Well, I wonder why the other guy did it," Jennifer said. "Maybe we'll get to ask him about that."

That was one bad thing about Ray shooting Hamilton dead—though Hamilton had fired at Patterson first—nobody could ask him who he'd been with that day at the lake, or which one of them had strangled Jennifer's mother. It would have been logical for her mother to open her door to one of the men who was investigating her son's murder, but wouldn't he have just gone to the driver's side?

Hamilton was dead, and couldn't tell them anything. But there had been two guns fired that day at the lake, two different calibers of bullet that ripped through her brother. Maybe the other shooter was gone. Maybe he was still here. She didn't know.

The one thing she did think she knew, though, was that Hamilton hadn't been the one to hang those pictures on her bedroom wall. She'd seen it in his face. Ray doubted her certainty, she knew. Ray was hoping Hamilton was the only one of the two that had still been around, though he didn't say as much.

"I'm gonna head out," Daniel said behind her.

Jennifer and Inez both turned.

"Are you sure you don't want to stay for dinner?" Jennifer asked, but she knew he'd say no again. Things had been even more awkward between them the last two days.

"Thanks, but I'm just gonna go home and get some rest," he said. He paused for a second. "Could I talk to you for a minute, though?

"Sure," Jennifer said, a twist of dread running through her stomach. They were going to have a talk. "Let me just wash my hands."

Daniel nodded distractedly. "See you later, Inez."

"See ya, Daniel."

He went back out of the kitchen, and Jennifer turned on the faucet, squeezed some dish soap into her hands.

"Don't be so scared," Inez said softly, not looking at her.

"I'm not scared," Jennifer lied.

"Sure, you are. You're still in love with him, and that's scary."

Jennifer swallowed and rubbed at her hands underneath the running water. "I was too old to stay in love with an eighteen-year-old boy," she said sadly.

She turned off the water and rubbed her hands on her butt. "But I think I fell in love with the man, and that's even scarier."

She walked out of the kitchen without waiting to hear what Inez had to say about that.

Daniel was standing on the front porch, his hands on the rail, looking out at the yard. He looked over his shoulder as she came through the screen door and let it shut behind her. She went to stand beside him, leaned her hip on the post.

"You need a dog," he said.

"I don't want a dog."

"You probably don't want deadbolts to lose the keys to, either, but there you go," he answered.

"I won't lose them."

He rolled his eyes. He'd known her most of her life. "I have an extra set for when you do."

They were quiet for a minute. Daniel pulled a toothpick from his shirt pocket, turned it around a few times, then put it back and looked at her.

"I'm sorry. For the way I did that, the other day."

Jennifer just looked at him. She didn't know what to say to that, even though she'd been expecting to hear it, or something like it.

He shook his head. "I was trying to think fast and that's what I got," he said. "But I saw…I saw the way you looked before you realized, and I'm sorry for it."

"Don't be," she said, her voice smaller than she'd like.

"I wouldn't do something like that, to lead you on or make you think something was possible that wasn't."

She nodded. "I know."

He opened his mouth, then seemed to change his mind, and shut it again. "I just wanted to make sure you knew that."

"Okay." She desperately wanted him to leave. She desperately wanted him to stay.

"Okay. I'll see you in the morning."

"See you later," she said.

She watched him walk down the steps. He stopped a little way down the path, and turned around.

"Not that I don't wish it was possible," he said quietly. "Sometimes I do."

He turned back around and walked quickly to his truck. She watched him go, the sun turning his golden-brown hair into fire. He climbed into his truck, then backed out and turned around without looking back at her. She blinked a few times to ward off any tears that thought about forming.

"It's good that you still love him," Grandma said behind her.

Jennifer turned to look. Grandma was sitting on the swing in her faded blue-flowered house dress and bare feet. She was looking at the Woman's Day magazine that was open on her lap.

"I don't know where you got that idea," Jennifer said. "It sure as hell doesn't feel good."

"Don't cuss, Jennifer Marie."

"Sorry."

Grandma looked up at her. "He's just hurting a bit, that's all, just like he always is when you have a set-to."

"We haven't had a set-to, Grandma."

"It'll be just fine."

Grandma smiled at her, and her smile was kind and understanding, the way it had been whenever Jennifer had been lonely or hurting or sad. She could always go to Grandma, if Jonah wasn't around.

"I wish Jonah would talk to me the way you do," Jennifer said sadly.

"Well, Jonah always was kind of a quiet boy."

"For eighteen years, I felt him like he was inside me, and I was inside him. Now, there's just nothing."

Grandma looked up at her a minute. "No, not nothing," she said. "We are made up of all of the people we have ever loved."

Now Jennifer did blink away tears. She looked out at the yard where her mother had waved to the camera. Where Grandma had planted lilies and kalanchoe. Where she and Inez and Jonah had played, and where Daniel had kissed her for the first time.

"Good," she said.

THE END

Please keep reading for a sneak peek, Dawn Lee's other books, and contact info

THANK YOU SO MUCH FOR SPENDING YOUR TIME IN DISMAL, FLORIDA.

I HOPE YOU'VE ENJOYED IT. AN HONEST REVIEW WOULD BE MOST APPRECIATED.

ABOUT THE AUTHOR

Dawn Lee Mckenna is a Florida native, a child of the 60s and 70s, and a serial cancer-survivor. She currently lives in Tennessee, with five children, seven grandkids, and the dream of a farm.

Read Dawn Lee McKenna's bestselling Forgotten Coast Florida Suspense Series here.

THE FORGOTTEN COAST BOOKS, IN ORDER

Low Tide

Riptide

What Washes Up

Landfall

Dead Wake

Awash

Apparent Wind

Lake Morality

Squall Line

Overboard

Back of the Bayou, a Bennett Boudreaux/Miss Evangeline novella

Ebb Tide, a prequel novella

YOU MIGHT ALSO LIKE THE SPIN-OFF, THE STILL WATERS SUSPENSE SERIES, CO-WRITTEN WITH AXEL BLACKWELL

Dead Reckoning
Dead Center
Dead and Gone

You can follow Dawn Lee McKenna on Facebook or subscribe to her mailing list, to get heads-up on new releases, special events, and appearances.

SPECIAL THANKS

Special Thanks to Colleen Sheehan of Ampersand Book Interiors, Shayne Rutherford of Wicked Good Book Covers

Heartfelt thanks also go out to beta-reading team Meg Trigg, Mike Keevil, Linda Maxwell, Vivian Edmonston, Jill Rowland Meister and John VanVelzor.

You are so deeply appreciated

If you haven't read the bestselling Forgotten Coast, Florida Suspense series yet, here's a sneak peek at the first book, Low Tide

LOW TIDE

SNEAK PEEK

The seagulls bounced around him, lighting just long enough to snatch up the pieces of bread, then hovering in the air, wings whipping, to wait for more.

Gulls were mercenary and self-absorbed, but he liked them. They were honest about their selfishness, unafraid of disapproval. At the same time, they were beautiful and graceful and they were the sight and sound of home.

He'd spent his entire life in Apalachicola and on St. George Island, just a few miles from the coast across the causeway. To his mind, it was one of the few places left that actually felt like Florida, with its century-old brick and clapboard shops and houses, the marina filled with shrimp and oyster boats and people who couldn't care less about Disney World.

Every time he'd left the Panhandle, for college or just to escape, he'd always felt slightly lost. Cities and nightlife and people with unfamiliar last names quickly lost their luster. Whenever he'd arrived home, after a few weeks or a few years, he'd felt his lungs open up to the salt and the heat and he'd known that he hadn't really breathed since he'd left.

Always, he came here first, to this virtually undisturbed, unblemished part of the island that was now a state park. Here, he could be the only sign of humanity among the white dunes and the sea grasses and the gulls and crabs that lived among them. Looking out to the ocean, he felt at once humbled and comforted by his own unimportance.

This was his sanctuary, his place of respite and refreshment. Here, there were no problems; there were no decisions or responsibilities or agendas. He could come here and empty his mind. He could fill his lungs with great, hungry breaths of salty air and be renewed, then go back to the mainland stronger, calmer, more ready to deal with his life and the people in it.

A gust of early-summer wind snatched at the plastic bag of bread, winding it around his wrist and causing the hovering seagulls to reverse themselves in the air, putting a few feet of distance between them and him. He unwrapped the almost-empty bag from his wrist and the gulls moved back in as he tossed out a few more pieces of crust.

He often felt like this group of gulls was the same group that he'd fed every time he'd ever come, the same birds he'd fed when he was ten or twenty. He felt like they remembered him, knew him and waited here for him when he was gone. They were his friends, really, or so he felt. They made him happy, with their flapping and grabbing and screeching.

He tossed out the last of the bread and the gulls landed in perfect synchronicity, like one being. He stuffed the bag in the left pocket of his khakis so that it wouldn't be a danger to the sea creatures, then pulled the gun from his waistband and slowly sat down on the sand.

A few minutes later, the explosion from the gun sent the gulls screeching into the air, then gradually, tentatively, they all came back to the sand. The ones with blood splattered on their gray and white bodies seemed especially agitated, even for seagulls.

Maggie Redmond pulled the coverlet over her head as her cell phone bleated from the nightstand.

"No," she grumbled from under the covers, but the bleating continued and the coverlet did little to block the late morning sun.

She snaked a hand out from under the covers and pulled the cell phone in, thumbing the *answer* button.

"I just went to bed. If this isn't life threatening, hang up."

"No," she heard Wyatt Hamilton rumble back. Wyatt was the Sheriff of Franklin County and her boss. "I need you to come over to St. George Island. Got a guy that shot himself on the beach."

"So? How badly is he hurt?"

"I don't know how bad it hurt, but it sure as hell killed him," Wyatt said.

"Ugh. Did you tell him it was my first day off in two weeks?"

"I mentioned it," he answered. "We're at the first pull-off before you get to the state park."

"Do I have time to take a shower?"

"Well, he's awfully close to the shoreline and the seagulls keep making off with chunks of his childhood memories, but you're the investigator, so it's your call."

"Alright. Stop it," Maggie said, throwing her legs over the side of the bed. "Give me thirty minutes."

"Okay," Wyatt told her. "I know you're gonna stop at Café Con Leche. Bring me one."

"Do you have an ID?" Maggie asked as she stood up and pinched at her eyes.

"Yeah. Gregory Boudreaux," Wyatt answered, then hung up.

It took Maggie a minute to put the phone down on the bed. It also took her a minute to remember to exhale. She walked into the bathroom and turned on the cold water tap. She splashed a couple of handfuls of water onto her face and stood and looked in the mirror.

Then she leaned over and threw up into the toilet.

Getting to St. George Island by car involved taking US 98, a five-mile or so causeway across East Bay to Eastpoint, then taking 300, another causeway that seemed to run four miles out into the Gulf of Mexico and stop, but which actually ended at St. George.

There were days like today, when cloud cover was low, that Maggie got the impression she was driving out to some distant point on the horizon, leaving the mainland behind her for good. Off to her left was Dog Island, a state preserve with more egrets and gators than people. To her right was Cape St. George Island State Preserve, just a few yards of ocean from St. George itself.

Maggie rolled her window down and breathed deeply of the thick, salty air. She was driving straight into the morning sun and it scalded her eyes, already dry and tender from lack of sleep. She'd left her sunglasses at home, so she blinked several times to soothe her eyes and pulled the visor down.

Arriving on St. George, Maggie continued on 300, which turned into a main drag of sorts, running parallel to the beach and attended to on either side by streams of vacation rentals in various pastels. St. George Island was about 28-miles long and around half a mile wide in most places. The southern eight miles of the island made up the State Park.

After just a couple of miles, she passed through Vacationland and into the stretch of road leading to the 2,000-acre State Park. After half a mile, she came to the pull-off, a spot of asphalt with five or six parking spaces, all of them occupied.

Today, the spots weren't filled with trucks belonging to men doing a little shore fishing. There was Wyatt's cruiser, another car from the Sheriff's department, the Medical Examiner's van, and an apparently unnecessary EMT truck.

Finally, there was a blue Saab that Maggie knew belonged to Gregory Boudreaux, who was reportedly losing his mind on the beach.

Wyatt was leaning against his cruiser when Maggie pulled in. He headed over to Maggie's ten-year old Cherokee as she parked and got out. He was easily six-foot four and, though he was closer to fifty than he was forty, walked toward Maggie's Jeep with the lanky, relaxed gait of a man half his age.

Wyatt had come to Apalachicola from Cocoa Beach a little over six years ago, following his wife's death from breast cancer. Between his widower status, the tinge of gray in his light brown hair and mustache, and his bright blue eyes, he'd quickly become the unconcerned darling of the women of Franklin County. His combination of goofy, self-deprecating humor and movie star looks made him equally popular with men and women.

Maggie knew that, his laid-back approach notwithstanding, Wyatt was smart as a whip and actually took his job pretty seriously, despite the fact that Apalachicola's crime rate made Cocoa Beach look like Detroit.

She grabbed Wyatt's coffee and handed it to him as the wind whipped her long, dark brown hair around her head.

"So, what's the story?" she asked as she yanked her hair into a ponytail.

Wyatt took an appreciative swallow of his coffee before answering.

"Vacationite by the name of Richard Drummond found the body at 8:15 while he was walking his dog. A Golden Retriever mix of some kind. Might be a little Lab in there."

Maggie grabbed her coffee out of the console, handed it to Wyatt and slammed her door before heading to the back of the Jeep.

"When did Larry get here?" she asked, referring to the medical examiner.

She opened the gate and pulled out her crime scene kit.

"About ten minutes ago," Wyatt answered. "He's talking to the deceased now."

"Who got here first?" she asked him, squinting over at the other cruiser.

"Dwight got the call from dispatch, got here at 8:25," Wyatt said. "He called me on the way and I got here a little after 8:30."

He took another swallow of his coffee and held hers out to her.

"No one else has happened on the scene and Dwight's got it taped off. I took lots of pretty pictures for you."

Maggie reclaimed her coffee and took a long swallow before they started walking the twenty or so yards along the path through the sea oats. Wyatt was more than a foot taller than Maggie and she took two steps to his one.

"Are we sure it's suicide?"

"'course not," Wyatt answered. "That's why you're here."

"Couldn't you get Terry to handle it?"

"He's over in Eastpoint working that robbery," Wyatt said. "That's what happens when you're fifty percent of the Criminal Investigation Division, Maggie. You want guaranteed days off, move to Tallahassee."

They reached the beach and Maggie saw the scene about ten feet further east. Larry Wainwright, a hundred years old if he was a day, was perched gingerly in the sand and leaning over the body. Sgt. Dwight Shultz, also known as Dudley Do-right, was keeping the seagulls out of the way by tossing them potato chips a few yards down the beach. The two EMTs stood nearby, with nothing really to do but wait to be dismissed.

Maggie and Wyatt stepped over the yellow crime scene tape and stopped near Gregory Boudreaux's splayed and loafered feet.

"Morning, Maggie," Larry said over his shoulder.

"Morning, Larry," she answered. "So what do we know so far?"

"Well, rigor's set in the face. It is now 9:20," Larry answered, checking his watch. "Between that and body temperature, I'd say time of death was between 6:00a.m.and 6:30."

Maggie finished pulling on her Latex gloves and crouched on the other side of the body with a few baggies in her hand.

A .38 revolver lay next to Gregory Boudreaux's right hand, his thumb still stuck in the trigger guard. She glanced over at Larry.

"Wounds seem consistent with a .38?"

"They do," Larry answered, and gently placed a gloved finger on the chin to turn the face toward him. "As you can see, we have quite the exit wound, which we'd expect from something of that caliber."

"So it appears to be self-inflicted then?"

"I'd say so at this point. I don't see anything at this juncture to argue against it," Larry told her. "As you can see, there's quite a bit of blowback on both hands, as well as residue."

"Kind of unusual, it being so close to the body," Wyatt mentioned noncommittally.

"True, true," said Larry. "The kickback will usually send it flying. But I'd say it stays nearby or even in the decedent's hands about twenty percent of the time."

"You know Gregory Boudreaux, Maggie?" Wyatt asked her.

"Some," she said.

"Can you think of any reason he might want to blow his brains out?"

"I can't really think of any reason why he shouldn't," she said evenly, focusing on Gregory's lifeless right hand. There was a good bit of blood splatter.

"Well, then," Wyatt said. "Can you sugarcoat that more specifically?"

Maggie took a slow breath and removed Boudreaux's thumb from the trigger guard and placed the revolver in an evidence bag. She breathed out only after she'd sealed the bag.

"Not really," she answered finally. "He was just your average Boudreaux, entitled and self-absorbed."

The medical examiner struggled to rise and Wyatt hurried over to give him a hand.

"I've got what I need in the immediate," Larry told them. "I'll take one of those responder boys back to the van to get the body bag. Once we get him up, you'll find most of the rest of the skull fragments are underneath his shoulders. Indicates to me he was seated when the gun was fired. I'll know more in a couple of days."

Larry called for one of the EMTs to come get a body bag, and Maggie watched the old man make his way back toward the parking area before she squinted up at Wyatt.

"Where's the guy that found him?"

"I told him he could go on back to his rental," Wyatt answered. "I took his initial statement. He and the dog left the rental for their walk about 8:00, according to the *Today* show. He didn't hear anything unusual prior to that, no gunshot or anything. You want to talk to him when you're done?"

"How long is he here for?"

"He checks out of the rental on Monday."

"I'll wait. So far, it looks like a straight suicide. I don't see any reason – was there a note?"

"Not so far. Checked his car, but I didn't check his pockets."

Maggie looked down at the body and sighed.

"Getting squeamish in your old age?" Wyatt asked her with a quick smile. She'd only just turned thirty-seven.

Maggie shot him a look, then reached into the right front pocket of Boudreaux's khakis. A set of keys to the Saab and a stick of Dentyne. She bagged them and reached over the body to the other pocket, pulled out the empty bread bag.

Maggie and Wyatt exchanged a look and Maggie looked back toward the path to the parking lot.

"Well, I don't think he left a trail back to his car," Maggie said.

"Dwight said it looked like he'd been feeding the gulls. When he first got here, there were a couple of birds with some splatter on them."

Maggie looked over at Dwight, who had run out of potato chips and was shaking the bag at the remaining few birds, yelling, "Git!"

"Dwight, you think he was feeding the birds?" she called, holding up the bread bag.

"Wouldn't surprise me," he said, flapping his arms. "He liked to come out here a lot."

Maggie frowned at Dwight's back.

"How well did you know him?" she asked. Dwight looked over his shoulder at her.

"I didn't, really," he said. "But back when my brother Rob was still drinking, they used to hang out from time to time. They came out here to fish quite a bit and he told me once that Boudreaux almost always brought something for the seagulls. It bugged Rob, 'cause they'd hang around and try to get at the bait."

"Okay," Maggie said and bagged the bag. Then she looked at the body for a minute before looking just past the head, where a few bits and pieces of skull and hair had been glued to the sand by tacky blood. She looked back at the dead, meticulously manicured hands, and stretched her neck to conceal the shiver that went up her spine.

"Would you mind bagging the hands for me while I get what's on the sand there?" she asked Wyatt.

"Sure."

Wyatt squatted on the other side of the body and set his coffee down behind him while Maggie took some baggies and tape out of her kit. She handed them to him.

"Thanks," she said, not looking up at his face.

She pulled a folding shovel out of her kit, opened it up, grabbed a few more bags and gently scooped up the remains and some sand, placed them in bags without talking further. As she slid the last scoop of sand and brain matter into a bag, a deformed .38 round revealed itself in the depression she'd left.

"Got a bullet," she told Wyatt and picked it up and dropped it into its own bag.

"Did you get to see your kids this morning?" Wyatt asked her.

"Only long enough to walk them to the school bus," she said.

"Sorry about your day off," Wyatt told her. "I know you needed it."

"It's okay," she answered. "I don't think this is going to amount to anything, do you?"

"Doesn't appear that way," he answered.

"Well, then I might still get tomorrow off," she said quietly. "I've got a bunch of squash and peppers to pick for tomorrow."

Two days a week, local gardeners brought produce to Battery Park next to the marina, to be distributed among oyster-fishing families still trying to recover from the latest oil spill. The oysters still hadn't come back to their former numbers and maybe they never would. They'd already been in decline, thanks to the two previous spills and Atlanta's insistence on stealing water from the Apalachicola River to fill its swimming pools.

"I'm assuming Bennett Boudreaux is the next of kin?" Wyatt asked as he handed Maggie her roll of tape.

Maggie looked up at the Sheriff.

"I would say so," she answered. "He was the only child of Boudreaux's only brother. His parents died when he was about twelve, I think. I don't know anything about the mother's family. They're in Mississippi or Texas, something like that."

"Well, notification should be fun," Wyatt answered. "Wanna come?"

"Yeah," Maggie answered distractedly.

"It's a Friday, which one of his businesses should we visit first?"

"He usually works out of the Sea-Fair office," Maggie answered, referring to the plant where Bennett Boudreaux bought, processed, and shipped oysters and Gulf shrimp. "But I hear he doesn't go in all that much anymore."

"Well, then let's try the house," Wyatt told her.

Larry and the EMT came back, carrying a gurney over the deep, powdery sand. They released the legs once they reached the body, and the medical examiner unfolded a black body bag and laid it next to the body.

When the EMTs lifted the body by the shoulders and feet, a small chunk of bloody skull dropped to the sand, joining several other bits of hairy bone in the bloodstained patch of sand that had been beneath Gregory Boudreaux.

It wasn't until the men had the body on the gurney and began zipping the bag that Maggie looked at the face. There were burn marks on one side of the open mouth, and the top teeth that remained looked almost out of place in the bloody mess that surrounded them. Gregory's eyes were closed, a fact for which Maggie was grateful.

Maggie felt a small wave of revulsion creep through her stomach. As the bag zipped shut over his face, she tried to summon some measure of human or at least professional sympathy, but the only thought that came to mind was, *Better late than never.*

For a town with one traffic light and a population of fewer than three-thousand people, Apalachicola had a preponderance of historic buildings. Between the old warehouses and quaint shops and cafes downtown along the bay and the residential historic district, there were around nine hundred buildings on the National Historic Register.

The architecture of Apalach was a mixture of Greek Revival and Florida Cracker, brick mansions and squat shotgun houses. Apalachicola often put visitors in mind of a Floridian version of Nantucket. There were quite a few people who had come from up north to spend a weekend and ended up retiring there. There was also a substantial artist community in town.

The result was a town that looked like it was stuck in the past, but which was actually surprisingly progressive in many ways. Fifth-generation oystermen with GEDs had lively discussions with former professors from Yale, and gay activists checked their event schedules with those of the DAR so that Battery Park didn't get overbooked.

Many of the most impressive old houses in town were located just a few blocks from downtown, on the Alphabet Avenues. Bennett Boudreaux's house was among them, on Avenue D.

Among other things, Bennett owned the largest seafood distribution company in Franklin County, shipping Apalach oysters as far west as Colorado and as far north as New York. He also owned trucking companies in both Apalach and Louisiana, several vacation rental houses on St. George, and a few local politicians.

Boudreaux's father had moved here from south Louisiana in the 1960s, gradually turning one oyster boat into a fleet and opening his own seafood business. Bennett had left Apalach to get a degree in finance at Ole Miss, then spent some years in Louisiana, building his businesses from the ground up. He'd come back to Apalach to take over his father's shipping business almost thirty years ago, when his daddy died of a massive coronary. Some people, when they weren't anywhere near Boudreaux, whispered that he'd probably scared the old man to death.

Boudreaux had never been convicted of anything in court, or even arrested for anything. However, he'd been convicted of many things in the minds of most of the law enforcement officers and many of the citizens of Franklin County. He was suspected of running drugs, interfering with unions, bribing judges, funding politicians, and even contracting the odd murder or missing person.

Boudreaux sat on numerous boards, sponsored many events, and even helped judge the oyster-eating contest at the annual Florida Seafood Festival, but more than a few people were more than a little scared of Bennett Boudreaux.

Maggie pulled her Cherokee into the oyster shell driveway in front of Boudreaux's two-story, white house, a wide, wooden home in the Low-Country Plantation style, which sat on a deep lot of almost an acre.

Maggie saw Wyatt pull his cruiser in behind her and she turned off her Jeep and climbed out. As Wyatt made his way over to her, Maggie looked at the front porch that extended all the way around the large but surprisingly unpretentious house. Pots of begonias in every color hung from the porch rafters and larger pots of hibiscus sat on either side of the steps. An array of white wrought iron chairs and tables filled the porch from one end to the other.

Wyatt met Maggie at her car.

"Nice place, huh?" He took off his sunglasses to look up at the house.

Maggie shrugged without commitment and they headed over to the flagstone path, oyster shells crunching beneath their feet. Once they got to the front door, they exchanged a look and Wyatt stepped forward. The white wrought iron screen door squeaked as he opened it to knock on the solid cypress front door. He eased it shut and waited.

A moment later, a light-skinned black woman opened the door and peered at them without much interest. She was in her mid-fifties or so, angular and tall in a flowered housedress and straw slippers. She wore a white half-apron over her dress and was drying her hands on a towel made of French ticking.

Maggie knew Amelia only by sight and only by first name. Boudreaux had brought her and her mother back from Louisiana with him, but no one ever saw the mother anymore and Amelia kept to herself.

"Yes?" Amelia asked them, her voice deep and sandy.

"Is Mr. Boudreaux available, please?" Wyatt asked. "We need to speak with him."

Amelia looked from Wyatt to Maggie, then cut her eyes toward the back of the house.

"Mr. Bennett out back with his mangoes," she told them. "You can walk around."

Wyatt nodded something like thanks, and he and Maggie walked back down the steps, the door closing quietly behind them.

They walked to the side of the house, where they picked up an oyster-shell path through excessively healthy bougainvillea and hibiscus bushes and ended up in a back yard that took up most of the deep, narrow lot.

Beyond a paved patio area just in back of the house, the rest of the lot was devoted to a dense planting of trees. There were coconut palms, bananas, Key Limes, oranges, avocados, and grapefruit, but the entire back of the lot was set aside for at least a dozen large mango trees. Mangoes weren't the easiest thing to grow this far north unless you had the money for heaters and tarps and other means of intervention. Boudreaux did.

In a sunny spot in front of the mango orchard were several rows of mangoes in various sizes and in various pots. This was where they found Bennett Boudreaux

Wearing tan cotton trousers and an untucked white shirt, he was picking yellowed leaves from a young potted tree. He wore dark sunglasses and a straw Panama hat with a yellow band. Wyatt and Maggie crossed the grass and stopped a few feet away.

"Mr. Boudreaux?" Wyatt asked.

Boudreaux looked over his shoulder. He was small in stature, maybe five foot seven, but a youthful and handsome man, even in his early sixties. He removed his sunglasses as he turned to face them, revealing brilliant blue eyes underneath his curious frown.

"Good morning, Sheriff," he said, his voice much deeper than his size led people to expect. Everything about him, from his demeanor to his bearing, made him seem like a much bigger man to those around him, especially those who were not in his good graces. He was unfailingly polite and not given to bluster, but there was a blue collar hardness to him, despite his wealth and education, that intimidated many.

Boudreaux's eyes fixed on Maggie's for just a moment.

"Maggie," he said with a quick nod. Maggie nodded back. "I doubt you've stopped in to say 'hello,'" he said. "Please tell me those boys haven't been messing around in the marina again."

A few weeks earlier, some teenaged boys with a surplus of courage and a deficit of sense had climbed the chain-link at Boudreaux's boat yard and had a little party on one of his shrimp boats. The parents had been more than happy to make restitution, probably relieved that Boudreaux hadn't stopped by personally to collect it.

"No, Mr. Boudreaux, I'm afraid we have some bad news," Wyatt said quietly.

Boudreaux looked Wyatt straight in the eye.

"What is it?"

"Your nephew Gregory's body was found on the beach over on St. George," Wyatt said. "Right now, it appears he shot himself. He's dead."

Maggie watched as Boudreaux's left eye narrowed a bit and he lifted his cleft chin, but there was no other physical evidence of emotion. None was expected; it wasn't his way.

"When did this happen?" Boudreaux asked after a moment.

"Early this morning," Wyatt answered. "About six, six-thirty."

Boudreaux tossed the leaves he was holding into a bucket, then took off his hat, crossed himself, and wiped a forearm across his brow. He looked at his hat for a minute. Wyatt and Maggie waited for him. When he looked up, Boudreaux's eyes were dry and sharp.

"And you think he killed himself," he stated.

"It looks that way, yes." Wyatt took off his sunglasses and wiped at the bridge of his nose. "Did he live here? Did you see him this morning?"

"No, he has a cottage over on Eleventh Street. 746 Eleventh Street," Boudreaux answered. "I think the last time I saw him…yes, it was Tuesday. He came by the warehouse."

"You know if he owned a .38 revolver?" Wyatt asked.

"I couldn't say for certain, but we all have firearms," Boudreaux answered. "I know he had a rifle; we hunt at least once or twice every fall."

"Do you know why your nephew might have wanted to kill himself, Mr. Boudreaux?" Wyatt asked.

Boudreaux took a minute as he squinted up into the mango trees. A drop of sweat coursed from his perfectly barbered hair onto his brow. He touched it away with one finger before looking back at Wyatt.

"I'll be direct with you, Sheriff Hamilton. Gregory didn't make much of an attempt at living."

"How do you mean?" Wyatt asked.

"I mean he was a failure at the few things he was motivated enough to try," Boudreaux answered. "Dropped out of Florida State, got dumped by the two women he proposed to, and probably would have been fired from his job if I didn't own the company."

"So you're not surprised to hear he might have killed himself?" Maggie asked.

Boudreaux turned his gaze to Maggie.

"I am surprised, but I'm not shocked," Boudreaux answered. "I don't care to speak ill of the dead, especially my own family, but Gregory's never been a happy person and most of his unhappiness was his own doing. He was forty years old, and had nothing that wasn't paid for by someone else."

Boudreaux looked from Maggie to Wyatt, then looked down at the ground.

"Even so," he said, "I probably could have done better with him."

"Did you get along alright?" Wyatt asked.

"I'm not that easy to get along with," Boudreaux answered simply.

He ran a hand through his still-thick, brown hair and put his hat back on, cleared his throat.

"Do you know when my nephew's body will be released to the family?"

"I can call and let you know," Maggie answered. "It shouldn't be more than a couple of days if everything's as straightforward as it seems."

Boudreaux looked at Maggie with a touch of gratitude in his eyes.

"Thank you, I'd appreciate that," he said. "Do you need me for anything else at the moment? I'd like to call Father Manero and see about a Mass."

"Do you mind if we take a look at his home, see if he left a note?" Wyatt asked.

"No. I have a spare key in my desk," Boudreaux answered.

"That's alright, we've got his," Wyatt said. "We'll put them back with his effects when we're through."

Boudreaux nodded his thanks, then looked at the ground again. Wyatt was about to say something when Boudreaux looked up and spoke.

"It does surprise me that he shot himself," he said. "Not that he ended his own life, but that he didn't use pills or something."

"Why do you say that?" Wyatt asked.

"Suicide is a cowardly act, but putting a gun in your mouth takes some courage," Boudreaux said.

He looked over at Maggie.

"Gregory didn't have a lot of that."

Made in the
USA
Columbia, SC

82109892R00159